A FAMILY'S PROMISE

CAROLYNE AARSEN

Misty Ridge
Publishing

CHAPTER ONE

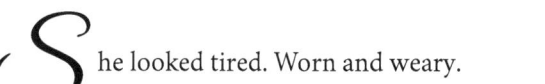

*S*he looked tired. Worn and weary.

Dodie slipped quietly into her mother-in-law's hospital room, draped her purse over the chair, and sat down beside the bed.

Kelly moaned in pain, her hand, lying on top of the bedsheets, twitching.

Dodie lifted it, holding it between hers, noting the veins, the bruises where the nurses had tried many times to start an I.V.

Bad veins, Dodie heard one nurse mumble as she tried the other hand.

Dodie brushed her hand over Kelly's, sending up a quick prayer for her dear mother-in-law. Kelly had endured so much over the past couple of years. And now she was recuperating from knee surgery.

As if sensing Dodie's presence, Kelly's eyes fluttered open, and she turned her head, smiling at Dodie.

"Hey, my dear," she whispered. "Thanks for coming."

"Has Dr. Page been by today?"

Kelly nodded. "He says I might go home next week once they get this infection under control."

"And then?"

"Then a home care nurse will come by and a physiotherapist until I can do my exercises on my own." She gave Dodie a warm look. "And that's where I'll be depending on you."

Dodie tried not to feel stressed by Kelly's words. Since she was told she needed surgery, Kelly had made no secret of what she hoped Dodie would be able to do for her. Increasingly, it sounded like being there for her 24/7.

Dodie had tried to explain that she was busy in her carpentry shop, working on a new commission that was important to her business.

So she said nothing, figuring she would deal with it as things came.

And how has that worked for you before?

The snide voice was a reminder of how Kelly could be a force to be reckoned with.

"You are the daughter I always wished I had," Kelly said, taking her hand. "I was always so thankful that you and Greg got married."

"Me too," Dodie said, her voice breaking at the mention of Greg's name. Though it had been almost two years, thoughts of her deceased husband could still bring out a surprising sorrow. Theirs wasn't a perfect marriage, but they had loved each other.

"And how was church yesterday?" Kelly asked. "Did you go?"

Dodie suppressed the usual guilt where church attendance was concerned. Sometimes she went, sometimes she didn't. Sometimes she plain forgot what day it was.

"No. I...I slept in," was the only excuse she could muster.

Kelly blinked then turned away, looking at the far wall of her room, her expression growing distant.

"Are you okay?" Dodie asked. "Are you worried about what will happen when you get home?"

"A little. It's kind of scary not to know what will happen, but, as always, I trust God will give me strength and peace."

Her mother-in-law's faith had always been an inspiration to Dodie. She often wished she could emulate her. But since Greg's death, and even before that, the events of her life had made it more difficult to build her relationship with God.

Kelly folded her hands on her stomach and swallowed. "I should let you know, I texted Cam yesterday."

A heavy silence followed her comment, followed by a flicker of anger as Kelly spoke Dodie's brother-in-law's name. Brother-in-law and ex-boyfriend.

Dodie didn't want to feel anything when it came to Cam Morgan. He was part of her past. A thoughtless mistake. Thank goodness Greg had been there for her and willing to take her back after that ill-fated relationship. She'd loved Greg deeply. He had been the best husband and partner she could wish for. He had given her stability, purpose, and a home in Millars Crossing.

Cam had just given her broken dreams and a broken heart.

"You don't look happy about it," Kelly said, frowning at her.

Dodie shrugged. "I've always had a hard time with Cam," was all she said.

"I understand, because I have as well. But he's my stepson, and I thought he should know what's going on. Besides, I'll need his help with decisions I have to make about the farm."

"Has he...has he texted you back?"

Kelly nodded. "He appreciated that I told him about my surgery. Said he hoped to come by some time."

"That was all?" His seeming callousness created a surge of anger. His stepmother was in the hospital and all he could offer was the "hope" of a visit.

She fought down her frustration, knowing it wouldn't help when, or rather, if, Cam came.

She didn't hold out much hope. Since he left all those years ago, she alternated between not thinking about him at all, then wondering what he was up to, then becoming angry as he crossed her thoughts. Cam had texted Greg once in a while those first few months. But after that, nothing. Greg never mentioned it, but Dodie knew Cam's silence bothered him.

"Did he say when he was coming?"

"Just that he would be here as soon as he could." Kelly shook her head sadly. "I tried so hard with that boy. I know I made mistakes, but I just wish we were closer." She looked tired, and Dodie couldn't stop a flare of anger with Cam. She knew his side of the story. The frustrated son who struggled with his stepmother. Dodie had taken his side at the time. Understood his pain.

But after they broke up, she got to hear another angle. Got to hear how hard Kelly tried to be a mother to a rebellious young man. Especially after his father died, and it plunged him into a deep grief. Kelly had tried to comfort and encourage him, but he rebuffed her at every turn.

Dodie brushed thoughts of Cam aside. The last few months she felt as if she had finally regained her balance after being tossed about by Greg's death. She didn't need any distractions. Right now, her focus was her mother-in-law and her needs.

"Of course you did," Dodie assured her. "You don't need to feel guilty about that."

Kelly took her hand again, closing it between hers. "I hope so. Maybe him coming here might help things."

"I should go. You look tired." Dodie got up and brushed a kiss over her forehead. "Did you want me to get you anything before I leave?" she asked. "A magazine or a book?"

"No. I'm fine." Another hint of a smile. "Though next time you come, you could bring me some treats from Adele's bakery."

"I'll see what I can bring," she said, giving her a gentle smile.

She knew she should go, but for some reason she was loathe to leave.

Just a few more minutes, she told herself. Then she would leave. Once Kelly was asleep.

SHE WAS EVEN MORE beautiful than he remembered.

More beautiful than any memory of her he had clung to those lonely times on the road. Sitting in bleak motel rooms picking at the strings of his guitar. Searching for a melody that was always just out of reach.

And always thinking of Dodie Westerveld. Correction, Dodie Morgan, widow of his stepbrother Greg.

Her dark hair still waved over her shoulders. Her profile could still steal his breath. High cheekbones, pert nose, soft lips, creamy skin.

Cam Morgan paused just outside the doorway of the hospital room, letting himself have a moment to put his ex-girlfriend in the proper place in his life.

The woman who wanted what he could never give her.

Cam ran a hand over his clean-shaven chin, smoothed his hair, reminding himself of another reason they were not together.

His stepmother who now lay in the hospital bed. Recuperating from knee surgery and a subsequent infection.

He pulled in a deep breath then stepped into the room, forcing a smile.

Dodie was the first to look his way. He saw the second she recognized him. Her hands clenched, her smile froze, and she retreated from him.

That cut like a knife.

But he knew he couldn't expect anything less after the way he broke up with her over six years ago.

The last time he'd seen her since then was at Greg's funeral two years ago.

Which had been an awkward affair. He had found out about Greg's death from a very brief text Dodie sent him giving him the information about the funeral—time and place. His reply ended the text string.

He had heard nothing from his stepmother.

At the funeral he wasn't sure where to go, so he sat down with the rest of the congregation in the church.

When the coffin came in, he couldn't hold back his tears. He had loved Greg and felt a true loss at his death.

But what tore at his heart was watching Dodie walking alongside his stepmother. Kelly leaned heavily on Dodie, her shoulders visibly shaking with sobs. Dodie looked thin, worn, and exhausted. It was all he could do not to run to her and help her. Support her.

But Dodie was the one who was being strong.

Dodie had helped Kelly to the family pew and sat down, draping her arm around her mother-in-law. Behind them came Kelly's sisters, a brother, and a few other people Cam didn't recognize. He clenched his fists at the injustice of it. At the pettiness of his stepmother at not making him part of the family.

When it came time for him to pay his respects, he gave Kelly what he thought would be a quick hug. But to his surprise, she leaned on him, sobbing on his shoulder. Then she pulled herself together and drew back. With her eyes intently on his, she told him how much she missed his brother, blinked a few times, then turned to the next person in line.

Next up was Dodie. Pale, thin, dark circles under her eyes, all accentuated by the black fitted dress she wore. She looked up at him, her expression haunted, and he had to fight not to sweep her into his arms, pick her up, and take her away. He shook her icy hand and was about to say something comforting to her when Kelly caught her arm, pulled her close, and introduced her to the couple behind Cam, cutting him out. Again.

So he left, his heart breaking and bruised. Receiving no consolation for his own loss.

He hadn't been back to Millars Crossing since. If it wasn't for the pleading text from Kelly, asking him to come, he wouldn't have bothered. But Kelly was in the hospital and it would look callous if he didn't at least make a token visit.

So here he was.

"Hello, Dodie," he said, hoping his voice held the casual tone he so badly wanted to project.

For a few seconds she said nothing, the silence like lead. Then she gave him a quick nod. "Hello, Cam."

Cam released a soft sigh, disappointment threading through him at her curt response. Not that he should be surprised. He had brought it on himself when he broke up with her. When he told her he couldn't give her what she wanted.

To stay in Millars Crossing and live on the farm and raise a family.

He turned his attention to Kelly lying on the bed, the sheet draped over her thin body, her eyes closed.

Frail was the first word that came to mind. Frail and diminished. She had always been a force to be reckoned with, but now, seeing her so wan, pale, and gaunt, her skin holding a grayish cast, he felt the first flickering of sympathy for her.

As if sensing his presence, her eyes fluttered open. She turned her head toward him and he received the same reaction he got from Dodie. Shuttering, a retreat.

She folded her bruised hands over her stomach, an IV snaking from the back of one. "So you came after all," she rasped.

Cam ignored the "after all." He had come as soon as he could. He was traveling with his band, Sons of the Homesteaders, on the last gig of this tour. So it'd been a couple of days before he could make the trip here.

He wasn't sure how to greet Kelly. He had never been affectionate with her. They had never been close. But he felt like he should do more than just stand there.

Besides, he sensed Dodie's expectations washing over him.

So he did something he had never done before. He brushed a gentle kiss over the papery skin of Kelly's forehead.

"How are you doing?" he asked. No sooner had the words left his mouth that he felt like smacking himself on the forehead. What a stupid question to ask of a woman lying in the hospital.

She gave him a wry look. "I'm recuperating from surgery."

"I'm sorry," he said. The old awkwardness that had hung like a heavy shadow between them returned with a vengeance. He always thought of himself as a self-confident person, but somehow around his stepmother that confidence was stripped away.

Cam was twelve the day his father introduced Kelly and her ten-year-old son Greg to him, three years after his mother passed away. Six months later, his father and Kelly got married. She and Greg moved in, and Cam had to share his father and his home.

At first things flowed along quite comfortably. His father doted on Kelly, who seemed to adore him just as much. He and Greg enjoyed each other's company. Cam was thankful for a playmate and someone who seemed to look up to him. He was also thankful for a mother, something he hadn't had for years.

But slowly one thing became apparent. Greg was Kelly's biological son and her emotional priority. On one level, Cam understood that. But the part that missed his mother yearned for more than the affection Kelly parceled out to him in dribs and drabs.

"And how are you?" she rasped.

"I'm good," was all he could manage.

"You still on the road steady with that singing group of yours?"

"I'm done for the next six or so weeks." He didn't want to say more than that. Not with Dodie standing there.

"So just hanging around."

Things are going gangbusters as usual, he thought. Shoved his hands in the pockets of his faded blue jeans, rocked back and forth on his booted feet.

His fellow band members always teased him about being the only authentic cowboy in the group. The only one who, when they sang about riding the range or hanging up the roping saddle, had some inkling of what that all entailed. And who had actually had a homesteader in his history. A couple of them were originally from Millars Crossing, but had been "town" boys.

Now he scrambled around, trying to think of the next question to ask. When Kelly looked away and closed her eyes, he wasn't sure if that was a dismissal or if she was just tired.

He went with the latter and turned to Dodie. Even with her glossy dark hair swept up in a sloppy topknot, a loose plaid shirt over a stained T-shirt tucked into slim-fitting blue jeans, she still looked amazing as she ever had.

Their eyes held and locked for a moment, and to his dismay it all came back so easily. The attraction he had always felt for her.

Dodie gave him a smile now. "And how is your band doing? I heard rumors you might do a world tour in the future."

"Just rumors for now. That takes a ton of organizing."

"I'm happy for you," she said, her soft lips shifting into a careful smile. "I know you poured your heart and soul into that band. Glad to know things are going well for you."

He was surprised that she even knew what was going on with him. Other than the funeral, the last time they spoke was during their breakup. When he said he couldn't marry her. The sight of the tears glistening on her cheeks was almost his undoing. Her anger washing over him was hard to bear. But he held firm despite the furious two-handed shove she gave him just before she spun around and strode out of his life.

But not out of his heart.

"So when does that happen? This world tour?" His step-mother's voice punctured the moment between him and Dodie.

He didn't think Kelly had been listening, but he should have known better. Not much slipped past her, even now.

"Our manager is working on it," he said, turning back to her. "I'll find out in a couple of months or so."

She released a hard laugh. "You always were chasing dreams. Now you get to do it around the world."

"Dreams are good to have," he said, adopting a casual tone, wishing her dismissal of him didn't matter so much.

Trouble was, since she had come into his life, he was always hoping for some scrap of approval from her. Some recognition of who he was. She had been kind at first. Willing to take him into her life. However, over time things shifted. Their personalities clashed. The fights got more heated. And his father consistently chose his wife over his son.

"So how long are you sticking around for?" Kelly asked.

"About two weeks. I'm headed to Mexico after this." Something he'd been looking forward to for the past half year of steady concert dates and moving around the country chasing gigs and money. He needed some downtime to reconnect with his muse. Find inspiration for the music that seemed to have dried up the past few years. "I know it's not long, but I'll stop in again after my trip."

"No, it isn't very long." Kelly paused, then struggled to pull in a breath. "But while you're here, maybe you can help me and Dodie out."

"Help you and Dodie with what?"

"Getting things sorted on the farm."

"Sorted? What are you talking about?"

Kelly drew in another shaky breath, winced, then looked over at him. "I'm selling the farm."

Cam could only stare at her, the news crashing into his world like a rock. Sending waves that reverberated to the depths of his soul.

"You're selling my dad's farm?"

Kelly's expression grew hard, her eyes narrowed. "I'm selling *my* farm," she returned.

Every cell in him wanted to shout that this wasn't true. Tell her it wasn't her farm. Never had been.

But, unfortunately for him, from a legal standpoint, her claim was true.

"That's hard to hear." Hard to speak past the surprising

and unwelcome thickening of his throat. He clenched his fists, willing the unexpected and unwelcome sorrow and anger away. He had worked this farm with his father for so many years. It had been his lifeblood. Had been the only thing he wanted to do at one time. At one time, it was to be his future.

"It is too bad," she said. "But Dodie can't afford it and, I imagine, neither can you."

For a tiny moment, Cam tested the idea. Could he buy back his father's farm?

But he pushed the ludicrous thought down, almost laughing at the irony of the situation. Wishing he'd taken better care of his interests. Not trusted his father to watch out for them. "No. I can't," he said. "Not now anyway." He had some money stashed away. After the North American tour it would be more.

Maybe...

She held his eyes a moment, as if looking for some deeper meaning to his words. Then she looked away. "I'm tired," she said.

"I'll be back tomorrow," he said, touching her hand.

"I'm leaving as well." Dodie came around the bed and gave Kelly a quick kiss.

His stepmother nodded, gave Dodie a warm smile, then closed her eyes.

Cam got the hint and followed Dodie out of the room.

A heavy silence dragged behind them, and while part of him wanted to hurry along, leave her behind, he knew how that would look. Like he was doing exactly what she had accused him of all those years ago.

Outrunning his responsibilities. Leading her on, then dropping her like she didn't matter.

"Do you have a place to stay?" Dodie finally asked as they

walked down the polished floors of the hospital, heading to the exit.

"Angie Flikkema runs an AirBnb. I'm staying there."

She gave a tight nod. "That's a cozy place."

"It's better than staying in a hotel," he agreed.

It was in town and, like Dodie said, it was comfortable and welcoming. It was a gigantic step above some places he and his band had stayed when they were scrabbling for gigs, taking just about anything that came their way, trying to save a few dollars by bunking together.

In this place, he had space and a kitchen to himself.

When he first talked about coming, he had floated the idea past Kelly of staying in his old room on the farm, but she had nixed it, saying she preferred her privacy.

Just one more of her many snubs.

"Just so you know, you don't have to help with the farm stuff," Dodie said when they got to the exit. "Kelly hasn't formally put it up for sale yet. She just wanted me to clear things out so it wouldn't be such a rush."

Cam pulled the door open for her and followed her out.

"I'll see how things go," he said, unable to say more. Though part of him wasn't sure he wanted to be involved with helping Dodie, he wanted to say a proper goodbye to his old home.

Maybe gather a few mementoes of his time there.

A way of saying a last goodbye in more ways than one.

CHAPTER TWO

*D*odie laid her head back against the headrest of her truck, disappointed at the pain that came back when Cam entered the hospital room. Seeing him again brought back a tangle of emotions. A vivid reminder of losing Greg.

They'd been so in love. So happy. And he was taken far too soon.

She swallowed down a knot of pain and pulled in a deep breath, swiping the tears away from her face, frustrated that they so easily came back after all this time. Her sister Janie had told her she had to find her own way through the grief. And mostly she had. She was feeling happier, freer than she'd felt in a while. Thoughts of Greg brought a smile and, occasionally, a tear.

But behind that came the complicated sorrow Cam created in her. He was in her past, but when he walked into the hospital room too many old emotions tumbled back, squeezed her bruised heart.

And now he was back for two weeks. She blew out a sigh, drawing on the old emotions she had buried deep. The anger and sense of betrayal he created in her.

The guilt.

She pulled out a tissue and blew her nose, pulling in a steady breath. It would pass.

It always did.

She put her truck in gear and drove away from the hospital. She had to pick up some groceries, a few more woodworking supplies, and then back to the cabin. The weariness that had dogged her ever since Kelly's hospitalization and the complications from it pulled at her. All she wanted to do was drop onto her couch, drink some hot chocolate, and binge watch some television.

But on her way home she drove past her sister's café. Though it was closed, there were still lights on inside. Maybe Janie was still working. Right now she could use a talk with her sister.

She parked in the back and punched in the code to open the back door.

Janie was singing some off-key song from church as she wiped down the huge butcher block workspace that took up most of the back room. Dodie could still feel the heat of the ovens as she walked past them.

"Yikes, girl," Janie called out as she looked up and saw her sister. "You scared the living daylights out of me."

"Living daylights? How does one even possess such a thing?" Dodie teased as she leaned on the counter. "And why are they never dying daylights? Or living nightlights?"

"Don't start with me. And I just cleaned that counter." Janie snapped the cloth she'd been using in her sister's direction.

"I'll clean it after. My elbows aren't that dirty. This is a clean shirt."

"And an improvement over that ratty thing I saw you in last."

Dodie didn't bother pointing out that ratty thing was one of Greg's old shirts. It made her feel close to him when she wore it. Connected.

But today she wore one of her own shirts, knowing Kelly would recognize if she wore one of Greg's. After all, Kelly had bought most of them.

"I'm not trying to win any fashion awards."

"Don't worry. You won't. Besides, one has to actually go out more often than you do to be even considered for any best-dressed list."

Dodie just shrugged at her comment.

The first few months after Greg's death she had kept to herself, hadn't taken care of herself. Janie and her mother would come and tidy the house and take her for a walk.

While they understood her grief on one level, they didn't truly get it, and it was too much work to explain her complicated emotions.

But slowly she emerged. Not the same carefree Dodie as before, but a reasonable facsimile thereof.

"How was the day at Coffee on the Corner?" Dodie asked, straightening, looking around to see if there was anything she could help her sister with.

"We were swamped today. That's why I'm still here. Thankfully Luke is on supper and kid duty tonight and told me there was no rush. So I'm not rushing." Janie gave Dodie a quick smile. "With the three kids at home, I take my moments where I can even if it means staying here after work."

"Why was it so busy?"

"A tour bus came through. He'd made a wrong turn but

parked the unit at the church and the people walked around town. Got a lot of people from that. Turns out they might do it again, so that's a good thing."

Dodie wrinkled her nose. "As long as Millars Crossing doesn't become another tourist attraction."

"What, you don't want people canoeing on your precious lake?"

"No. As a matter of fact, I don't. There's been a couple of loons that have made it their home, and they serenade me every night I go out on the lake."

"Well, I don't think you need to worry about that yet. How's Kelly doing?"

"Today was a better day for her."

"Good to hear, but still. It must be hard to watch someone who was always so energetic be so weak." Janie tossed her cloth in the overflowing basket of laundry she had to take home.

"It is. But the doctor figures she's rounded the corner. She'll be out in a few more days."

Janie paused, leaning on the counter as well, across from her sister.

"Didn't you just clean that?" Dodie teased.

"Yeah, but you're finishing the job. So tell me. What's up?"

"What do you mean?"

"You look extra stressed."

"It's Kelly," Dodie said, hiding behind her mother-in-law's hospitalization

"Nothing else?"

Trust her sister to be able to look past her feeble attempt at subterfuge.

Another sigh flowed out of her. One, she suspected, of many more to come.

"Cam is back."

17

Janie's expression shifted just enough to show Dodie that her sister understood the implications of that statement.

"And. How are you with that?"

Dodie picked at a crack in her fingernail. She'd caught it on some lumber the other day while she was running the planer. She never could keep her nails long or looking clean. Something their fashionable mother had despaired of for years.

"I don't know. It's hard on Kelly. He wasn't always the easiest person for Kelly to raise."

"That's putting it kindly. He was a terror. At least what I knew of him."

"Pretty rough around the edges," Dodie admitted. "But him being around reminds me of Greg again." That much was true.

"I can imagine that makes things difficult. How long is he around for this time?" Thankfully Janie didn't press Dodie or challenge her reasons.

Dodie shrugged. "A couple of weeks and then he's off on a North American tour. He said something about his band heading out on a world tour after that."

"So, gone again and for a long, long time."

Janie's wry tone reminded Dodie of the first time Cam had left—"headed out"--as Kelly said, to chase his dreams. But not before shattering hers.

"Yeah, which is a good reminder of what Cam is like," Dodie said.

"And why would you need a reminder?" Janie's question was quiet, but Dodie heard the implications behind it. Reminding Dodie of the time she and Cam spent together after she and Greg broke up. When Cam's life was scattered and represented disorder.

"I need the reminder, because he's still Cam. And, unfortunately, he's as good-looking and charming as ever. And he's still not settling down."

"Oh you and your settling," Janie said with a chuckle. "I'm scared that one day we'll come up to your secluded cabin and find you turned into a tree with roots going all the way down to the lake."

Dodie chuckled at the thought. "I can't think of a better place to end up."

"I'm glad you're happy there and I'm glad you and Greg had good times there," Janie said, her voice growing serious, which meant she was heading down the same path their mother often did. "But one of these days you have to move on."

"It's only been two years," Dodie protested.

"I know, and I also know that grief can't be rushed. That it's different for different people and in different circumstances. But still..."

Her sister let her voice trail off, leaving Dodie to fill in the pause.

"I've got a few projects on the go," Dodie said, clenching her hands together to keep herself from picking more at her nails. "It's taken time for me to get working." She didn't want to add that there were many more layers to her grief. Losing Cam when he left. Then Greg's death. She wasn't sure she wanted anyone to engage her heart. Better to keep to herself and pursue her own ambitions.

The first six months after Greg's death, she didn't dare go into the workshop. That was where she found him after his aneurism burst. Lying on the floor. At first she thought he had fainted, but when she found out he wasn't...when she found out he was dead, after that, even looking at the workshop was like a knife in her heart.

His small insurance policy paid off the land and cabin they lived in and gave her enough money to get by the first year without having to work full-time, but then she'd needed an income. Though Kelly had often said she would help out, Dodie was determined to be self-sustaining.

So pride and the need for income had been enough to push her back to the workshop and back to work, making the custom canoes and kayaks she was known for. Her business was looking up, and she was pleased that she could support herself and pay for her gardening obsession.

"Have you thought about going back to school?" Janie pressed. "Finishing up that teaching degree you started."

"You sound like Mom."

"I'm not taking that as a negative," Janie said with a grin. "Having kids has made me appreciate Mom in a whole new light."

Dodie wasn't sure what to say to that. While she and her mother got along, she wasn't as close to her as Janie had become. Especially the past few years.

To Tilly Westerveld, Dodie was a sweet but airy-fairy disappointment. Molding canoes in her workshop when she could be guiding and molding young minds. Working with wood when she could be working with children.

But Dodie only went to school after Cam broke up with her to satisfy her parents. She did one year then quit.

She'd always liked woodworking, and her Uncle Sam, when he came back from his time in Toronto, had helped her get started.

"I'm not sure I want to go back to school." She hated to admit how much work even that one year had been for her. She wasn't a natural student and disliked how insecure schoolwork had made her.

"You know Uncle Morris would gladly take you on if you got your degree."

Dodie gave her a wry look. "Bad enough that he's got

Sarah working at the school. It would smack of nepotism if two of his nieces taught there."

"He's the principal. He gets to make the hiring and firing decisions."

"I love what I'm doing," Dodie said with more force than she'd intended. "It gives me a lot of satisfaction, so please, just stop."

Janie pushed herself away from the table and held up her hands. "Got it. Sorry." She gave Dodie an apologetic look. "I'm not trying to pressure you. Just encourage you to be all you can be."

Dodie gave her a forgiving smile. "I get it. I know I'm not living the life that Mom and Dad dreamed of, but I'm happy. And that's got to mean a lot."

But even as she spoke the words, she couldn't meet her sister's eyes.

Because, despite her brave words, the same unnamed dissatisfaction she'd been feeling lately still niggled at the edges of her thoughts.

The feeling that there was more to life than what she was living. That something was missing.

She wanted to blame it on Greg's death, but the truth was, she'd felt it even when he was alive. She'd longed for children and a stronger connection between her and Greg.

"I agree. That's a good thing, and I'm thankful that you've found your way through this valley you've been in the past while."

"I am too," Dodie said. She glanced at the clock behind her sister. "And you should get going. I imagine you don't want to take advantage of Luke's generosity."

"No. Especially considering he asked me to bring dessert and I have nothing left. I sold out of everything at five o'clock, and Adele at the bakery is out as well."

"Some type of sugar rush relay running rampant through Millars Crossing?" Dodie said with a grin.

"Oh that's bad," Janie groaned.

"Tooth Decay Decathlon?"

"You can stop now."

"Just getting started," Dodie said, following her sister out the back of the bakery.

They both got to their vehicles, but before Dodie got in, Janie pulled her close in a quick hug.

"What's that about?" Dodie asked, giving her sister a gentle smile.

Janie brushed a strand of Dodie's hair back from her face. "Just happy that you're doing better. I enjoy seeing you smile."

"I enjoy seeing me smile too," Dodie said.

"And I'm sorry I pushed you on that teacher thing. You've got to do what works best for you."

"It's taken me some time to get here, and I know Mom and Dad have only my best interests at heart. It's just that they don't meld. And they'll have to be okay with it."

This netted her another smile.

Dodie got in her truck and as she backed up, she glanced back to see Janie watching her.

But instead of the smile, she caught the look of concern. Of worry.

She tried not to think what that was about as she drove away.

But as she did, her mind slipped back remembering when she and Cam got together.

She and Greg had been dating since she was in seventh grade. Their mothers were close friends and had planned Greg and Dodie's wedding since Kelly and Greg first moved to Millars Crossing. Their relationship was meant to be.

Then, a year after graduation, Greg decided he didn't love

Dodie as much as he thought. That maybe they were together because of their mothers.

So he broke up with her to see if he would miss her. Of course he stayed in Millars Crossing. He had a farm to run, after all. Of course she saw him regularly.

Dodie was crushed. But then, after a couple of weeks of doodling his name in her diary, of drawing tears dripping down the margins, she snapped out of it. Realized she was better than this.

And Cam was right there, waiting for her.

He waited a month and then asked her out.

Dodie had been well aware of Cam's ongoing interest in her. When she came over to the Morgan farm, it seemed Cam always had some joke for her. Some joking comment. At the time he and his friends already had their band and he would tease her by writing up some silly song about her on the spot.

In fact, Greg had once said to Dodie, right in front of Cam, that his stepbrother had a crush on her.

Dodie had laughed, Greg had chuckled, but Cam just looked at her, not denying it at all.

So when he asked her out, she wasn't really surprised. If she was being honest with herself, part of her was flattered. And some small part of her she didn't want to acknowledge had always been attracted to him as well.

Cam made her feel better. He told her Greg wasn't good enough for her. Told her if Greg didn't think he loved her enough—the amazing, beautiful, and talented Dodie Westerveld—then Greg wasn't worth crying about.

Dodie looked into those soft brown eyes, heard his gruff voice promising her that he did love her. Always had.

And she gave in to his charm and her own hidden emotions and fell hard.

They made plans. They were going to farm together. Cam

and his band would do local gigs and eventually set up a sound studio so he could write songs about the farming he was doing. Dodie could set up a workshop for the woodworking she loved doing. She dreamed of the small house they would build. The children they would raise.

On the farm Cam's great-grandfather had homesteaded.

Then Cam's father died and two months later, Cam abruptly changed plans. He wanted to leave Millars Crossing. He didn't want to work on the family farm, the farm his great-grandparents had started.

He told her he didn't want to settle down here. Didn't want to stifle his creativity by farming. Which seemed strange to her. He had always been the one who did most of the farm work and always loved it.

But all that changed after his father died. She thought maybe the farm reminded Cam too much of him. That being there made him sad. He never talked much about his father. Whenever she tried to bring it up, he would get upset, so she left it alone.

Then in one devastating conversation he told her this wasn't working. He couldn't give her what she wanted. When he left, without a proper goodbye, he took a huge part of her heart and all of her dreams.

She thought her breakup with Greg was bad, but although she had dated Cam less time than Greg, she was more torn up about this.

Two months after Cam left, Greg came back to her. Told her what a mistake he had made. That he was a fool, and that he loved her. Dearly. That he wanted to settle in Millars Crossing on the farm and raise a family.

Dodie was torn. Sure, she had cared for Greg, but he had left her high and dry once.

Her mother told her not to be silly. Greg was what she wanted. Greg would give her security. Then Kelly chimed in, campaigning for Greg, reminding Dodie of their ongoing relationship.

Greg represented stability.

Cam was heading down the road with an old beat-up truck and two guitars.

And neither her mother nor Greg's mother approved of him.

So she married Greg. They rekindled their romance, but the shadow of her relationship with Cam always hung in the background. Which always made her feel guilty.

After Greg died, her thoughts would drift back to her time with Cam. And she would wonder what her life would have been like had she told Cam she didn't care. That she was going with him.

But each time, she balked. Thinking of leaving Millars Crossing was like a punch to her stomach. It was her home. Her family and community were here, and she needed that more than she realized.

And as she pulled up to her house, her cozy retreat, she knew it was still true. This was still home and always would be.

CAM HESITATED at the end of the driveway leading to his old home.

Was it wise to come back here? Dodie said she didn't need his help. And he hadn't told her he was coming here today. He wasn't sure if she would be here or not.

Would it be trespassing if no one else was here to catch him?

He was just going to have a look, walk around the yard, say a last goodbye, he told himself.

Though the farm wasn't listed yet (he had checked), he

knew once it went up for sale there would be a bidding frenzy. The land was fertile and yielded good crops, and land around here seldom came up for public sale. Most deals were made sitting around the coffee machine at the Ag Center, one farmer chatting with another. Or whoever rented the land often got first dibs.

Cam felt a clench at the thought of the farm moving into other hands. Though he hadn't been back for years, it still called to him. Still made him feel like he had a place he could return to when life on the road became too much. Gave him roots.

He rounded the last curve of the driveway edged by the heavy grove of spruce trees that had gotten even taller since he was here last.

And when he drove closer to the house, he saw Dodie's truck parked beside the tractor sitting outside the equipment shop.

He felt a curious lift of his heart followed by a reality check.

Old emotions, he told himself. Old crush.

He was four girlfriends and many years past having feelings for his brother's wife.

Besides, her well-deserved anger when he left reminded him he had no right to come back into her life. That and the fact that he still couldn't give her the life she wanted.

He parked his truck beside hers, noting the rusted panels and bald tires. Were things that tight for her? Didn't Kelly take better care of her son's widow?

Not your problem, he told himself as he got out.

He listened a moment, smiling at the sound of the wind sifting through the trees surrounding the house, shielding it from the farmyard. A bird sang, followed by another. Then he heard the *rat-a-tat* of a woodpecker.

The familiarity of the place wrapped itself around his

soul. No matter where he went, where he lived, this would always be home to him.

Until it's sold.

Reality pushed his daydreams aside. He was here to help Dodie get the place ready for that very event. In a few months it would be gone and he would have no claim to it.

He headed toward the shop, pushing his wayward thoughts aside. No need to indulge in bygones or might-have-beens. He had to deal with reality.

He followed the tinny noise of a radio playing in the shop. Country music.

Dodie stood by a red stand-up toolbox, her head bobbing in time to the singer crooning about living at the end of a dirt road as she sorted through a drawer. The music echoed in the large, cavernous space capable of housing two tractors the size of the one outside.

He wasn't sure how to approach her without scaring her, so he moved to one side so she would see him in her peripheral vision.

He could tell the moment she saw him. Her head flew up and her hands froze mid-motion.

"Hey there," he said, daring to move closer. "How's it going?"

She turned back to the tool cabinet and emitted a sigh. "I just started, and I realized I have no clue what I'm doing."

"What do you mean?" he asked, coming to join her.

"I got a list from the fellow who will do the farm sale. He suggested I separate the tools into different lots so I could get more money. But I don't know where to start or how to sort them."

He resisted the urge to remind her she hadn't wanted his help at first, and here she was, asking his advice.

"Reality is, you won't get a lot more by separating them. And it's a lot of work. I think just leave them all together."

Dodie heaved out a sigh of relief at that. "Thanks. That makes things easier. There's three of these cabinets," she said, shoving the drawer closed.

"Three?" When he and his father were working together, he only had one.

"Greg enjoyed buying tools. The shop back at our place has all kinds of them as well."

"For your woodworking?"

"You remember?"

That she even had to ask disturbed him. "I helped you build a canoe at your mom and dad's place."

And put up with Tilly Westerveld's disapproving looks and frowns. Cam knew the relationship between Dodie and her best friend's stepson underwhelmed Dodie's mother.

"Of course. I'm sorry. I forgot."

How could she have? That day was etched in his memory. It was when he dared to make plans for a future with the two of them. Sure they were still in their late teens, but the heart knows what the heart knows. And Cam had always known what he wanted.

To marry Dodie Westerveld. Live on this farm and have kids.

But he was too shy and uncertain and knew she was too young to talk about such serious things. Greg, however, had no compunction and had swooped in before Cam could work up the courage to ask her out. That their mothers encouraged Greg's cause didn't hurt. But when Greg broke up with her, he knew he wasn't waiting this time.

But they were both in a different place now. She a grieving widow and he on the cusp of stardom. Their paths had, at one time, gone in the same direction, but not anymore.

"I guess before we get too carried away I should ask if there's anything here you might want?" Dodie asked.

"Am I allowed?" He couldn't help the sharp tone of his voice.

"Of course you are. This used to be your home. I can't imagine that Kelly would have any objection to you going through and picking out what you want. She knows how attached you were to this place."

"Does she?"

Dodie shot him a surprised look, and he didn't bother enlightening her.

"Look, I know you're not too crazy about Kelly," she said. "But you need to know she's had nothing but good to say about you. She cared about you and worried about you, prayed for you."

Cam just stared at her, wondering if they were talking about the same woman.

"You look like you don't believe me," Dodie said, a faintly accusing note in her voice.

"Well, my experience has been different." He couldn't stop himself from speaking his truth. Either Kelly had changed a lot, which he doubted, or she had Dodie fooled, which he suspected was closer to the truth. Dodie was a trusting, caring, and sensitive person.

"I know she struggled with a relationship with you when she first came," Dodie continued, "but I'm sure you can see how hard it must have been for her. She was joining you and your father on your farm and wanted to be a family. And she was a good and loving mother-in-law to me." Dodie sounded defensive, and the last thing he wanted was to get into a disagreement with her. Of course Kelly had loved Dodie. Who wouldn't?

Besides, Dodie was married to the favored son.

"I'm sure she was," was all he would say. When Kelly first came into their home, he wanted to like her. He missed his mother, missed having a mother. And at first it had been

29

wonderful. Coming home to a house that smelled of a treat baking. Supper on the table every night instead of only when his father had the energy or when he had enough groceries to wrangle something decent together besides fried eggs or grilled cheese sandwiches.

Fresh vegetables that first year when she put in a garden. It was idyllic.

The change in their relationship, however, was slow and insidious. Greg getting out of some farm chores in order to help Kelly. Greg getting a brand-new saddle when he was fourteen, while Cam had to make do with his hand-me-down from his father. Because, well, Cam already had a saddle now, didn't he?

Better clothes, more of an allowance.

Kelly could always sound reasonable about the discrepancies, and his father, somehow, let it all go. When Cam would try to point out the unfairness of it all, his father would tell him he had to give Kelly and Greg grace. That it was their Christian duty to help them become part of the family.

Cam gave up when Greg was allowed to join the volleyball team while Cam had to help in the fields because he was better at it than Greg who grew up in the city. And we didn't want any equipment getting wrecked now, did we?

"Okay then, where did you want to start?" he asked, pushing aside the old memories.

Kelly was sick in the hospital and he would be gone in a couple of weeks.

He had to do for Dodie as his father always said. Give her grace. And what did it matter anymore? She was grieving for her husband, his stepbrother.

Dodie seemed to make it clear she didn't want to have much to do with him anymore.

CHAPTER THREE

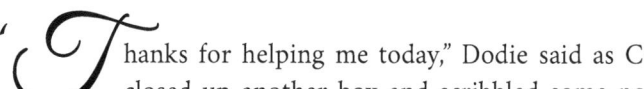

"Thanks for helping me today," Dodie said as Cam closed up another box and scribbled some notes on it describing what was inside.

This was the second day they'd been sorting stuff in the main workshop, and they had finished this building at least. Though she hadn't requested his help, she was glad of it now. "I've been putting it off for weeks, not sure where to start."

Cam, kneeling on the cement floor of the shop just nodded, then shoved the Sharpie in his pocket as he stood.

The collar of his shirt had gotten turned up in all the rearranging they had done the past few hours, and Dodie had to resist the urge to flip it down.

"You're looking at me funny," he said, brushing off the knees of his pants.

"Well, I wasn't going to say anything because I know how self-conscious you are," she teased, "But you've got a bunch of smudges on your face and your collar is crooked."

He frowned, then reached up and, holding her gaze, flipped the other side of his collar up.

His taunting made her want to smile, but also sent up warning bells.

She remembered when they were dating, and even before that, how he would show up half put together and she would straighten and tidy. Smooth his thick, wavy hair, re-button a shirt he had tossed on, adjust his tie the precious few times he wore one.

Cam never cared how he looked and now, with stubble shading his firm jaw, the streaks of dirt on his face, shirt, and pants, he looked like the old Cam. Not the one she saw in his promotional videos on YouTube or brooding at her from the magazine cover he'd been featured on. Sure, it wasn't a mainstream magazine, but it was still a cover and he still looked as dangerously appealing.

"Okay, very funny," she said, her fingers itching to put it straight.

"Sorry. Just messing with you." He straightened the collar and patted the points, looking to her. "Better?"

"Much better."

Their eyes held for a moment, but he was the first to look away.

"So the mechanic tools are sorted," Cam said, resting his hands on his hips as he looked around. "I know my dad had a bunch of woodworking tools. Drills and sanders."

"He did?" This was news to Dodie. "Greg never mentioned them."

"Really? I'm surprised. You have a woodshop on your yard. Surely you could have used some of them."

"Greg seldom worked in the shop back home. That was always my thing." But even as she excused her husband, she was surprised Greg had said nothing to her about his stepfather having woodworking tools.

"Dad even had a bunch of antique planers and drills we picked up at a farm sale."

"I'm sorry. I don't remember seeing them."

Cam looked around the now organized and cleaned-out shop. "I could try the red barn," he said. "They might be there."

Dodie frowned. "I don't think Greg ever put anything in there besides square hay bales for the horses when we had them."

But Cam wasn't put off by that. He left, striding across the grass to the two barns tucked side by side. One was much larger than the other and Dodie knew that one was often used for the cows when they were calving.

She would come and help Greg from time to time sorting cows, vaccinating them. Occasionally help when a cow was having a difficult birth. They'd had horses at one time, but Greg sold them a few years after they got married.

The horses were left over from when Cam was around but Greg wasn't much of a rider so he never encouraged Dodie in that either. Cropping the land and raising cattle was everything to him, so that became his only focus.

That and his occasional trips with his friends to Vegas to blow off steam in the fall at the end of harvest.

Not her style at all but it seemed to make him happy, so she put up with it. He never asked her along, which suited her fine. She much preferred to stay home.

Cam passed by the larger barn and went straight to the smaller of the two as she followed him. He grasped the huge handle of the door and pushed. The rollers squealed a protest as he shoved it open. He coughed as he disturbed who knew how many years of dust inside.

Dodie had never been in this barn. She looked around, surprised at how full it was.

"Here's the tack, something else I was wondering about."

Cam flicked on a light that gave a muted glow because of the dust coating the bare bulb.

Along one wall was saddle racks with four saddles resting on them.

"Did Greg never look after these?" Cam asked, running his finger over the liberal coating of dust on the one.

"Greg did some riding after we got married," Dodie said. "But not much."

Cam blew out a frustrated sigh as he lifted the saddle off the tree. "Mice got into the sheepskin on this one." He shook his head, moving to the one beside it. "And this one hasn't been oiled in years. How could he not have taken care of this?"

Dodie wasn't sure what to say to that. She could understand why Cam, who loved riding and spent much of his free time working with his horses, would be upset, but it wasn't Greg's thing. At all.

"He had a lot to do," she said in her husband's defense. "Taking care of the farm equipment was his priority. After all, it's the equipment-"

"It's the equipment that makes the money." Cam chimed in, giving her a wry look. "I sure got to hear that a lot the last few years I was here."

The harsh tone in his voice held a subtext she wasn't sure how to ferret out. Wasn't sure what he was trying to say. So again, she just held her tongue.

"Blankets, bridles, headstalls..." Cam lifted each in turn, shaking his head. "Why didn't he at least sell this stuff to someone who would have taken care of it?"

"Maybe because all this belonged to you and your father."

Cam shot her an annoyed look, but then his expression shifted and he nodded. "Sorry. You're right. Maybe he was waiting for me to come back and do something about it." He pulled in a deep breath. "But still. One of these is his own saddle he got brand new. It wasn't cheap either. At least he could have-" With a curt wave of his hand, he seemed to cut off his own comments. "Anyhow, it's done. I doubt we would get much for this at the farm sale. Does the Auction Mart still have a monthly horse sale?"

"Sorry. Again, not much of a horse person."

"I remember that. Should have pushed you a little harder to try though," he said, referring to the times he had urged her to come riding with him. They dated during the winter, so it had been more difficult to go. They'd gone a few times. But come spring he was busy in the fields working with Greg, and they hadn't wanted to flaunt their relationship.

And then his father died. And everything fell apart. Cam decided he didn't want to stay and farm. He wanted to make something of the music he'd been playing. The songs he'd been writing. The band he'd been playing with. And then he dropped a bombshell in her life. Told her he had to leave. That they had to break up. That he couldn't give her what she wanted. She pleaded with him to stay. To work on the farm, but he didn't listen. Told her had to make his own way in life.

She was devastated, heartbroken, angry, hurt. A storm of emotions she couldn't separate.

Then two months after Cam broke up with her, Greg came back into her life to comfort and console her. He said that Cam was never the type to settle down. And that he was sorry he had ever broken up with her.

Greg had been so caring and understanding, and she was at a loss. So with the encouragement of her mother and Greg's, she went back to him.

"Anyhow, I doubt any of this is worth putting up for sale." Cam crouched down by a stack of saddle pads, going through them, shaking his head.

Though the deterioration of the tack was not her fault or

her problem, Dodie felt responsible. She remembered asking Greg if they shouldn't do something with it all, but he dismissed it as unnecessary. The horses were gone, and this stuff was worthless. Besides, Cam might come back for it. So she'd left it.

But it wasn't hard to see the frustration and disappointment on Cam's face as he sorted and shifted.

"I might take this with me," he said, choosing one of the older saddles. "This one used to be my dad's."

"Of course," Dodie said. "You can take whatever you want." She realized how patronizing she sounded. Neither she nor Kelly had near the history of this place that Cam did, and now she was making it sound like he could take the crumbs.

But saying more would only draw attention to her comment, so she stood back, hands in her pockets as he set a saddle and a couple of bridles to one side.

"Trouble is, I don't have any place to store them for now," he said, pushing to his feet and turning to her. "Would it be too much trouble to bring them to your place until I leave?"

His last word rang in the silence, a potent reminder of what was coming.

"Sure. That's fine." It was the least she could do. "I'm sorry about the saddles," she said, feeling the need to apologize for something she had nothing to do with.

Cam held his hand up and shook his head. "It's not your fault. I just thought that Greg would..." He gave her a quick smile then looked past her.

"I see a couple toolboxes in the back there," he said, pointing. "I bet that's where my dad's tools are."

Dodie followed him, hoping he was right. Hoping these tools, at least, were in decent shape if they were indeed his father's. Cam opened the lid of one box and sat back, grinning. "Look at that. Perfect condition."

Relieved, Dodie moved closer, curious to have a better look.

"My dad liked to use the best tools." He pulled out a belt sander and grunted as he set it on the ground.

"That's a Makita," Dodie said. "I hope it still runs."

"Would you be interested in it?"

"You don't want it?"

Cam shook his head. "I don't think I'd have much use for a belt sander as I'm touring around." He added a light laugh, but Dodie couldn't help a small shiver of apprehension at the reminder of who he was and what was coming.

Him leaving again.

"No, I can't imagine you would," she said, bending down to have a closer look. It was dusty and could use some overhauling, but overall it looked almost brand new.

Cam was digging deeper in the toolbox. He pulled out another palm sander. "I imagine you'd want to keep this too," he said.

"I never say no to tools," Dodie said. "Though I should talk to Kelly about this."

At the mention of her mother-in-law's name, Cam narrowed his eyes. "I don't think you need to. These belonged to my father. Not her"

Dodie sensed she should leave it, but his reaction bothered her. "I know you've had your struggles with her-"

"Struggles?" His voice grew hard. "She was never the mother to me I needed."

"But she cared about you. She told me that herself. Told me she missed you and wished you would come and visit." She almost added that she did as well, but that would sound rather desperate, and besides, she'd thought about him more during her marriage to Greg than she should have. So best leave that be.

"She had a strange way of showing that caring," Cam returned.

"What do you mean?"

Cam waved off her question. "Doesn't matter. I know you get along well with her-"

"I love her almost as much as I love my own mother," Dodie said, struggling to understand. She saw Kelly in tears over Cam's lack of communication.

Something she could identify with.

"She missed you so much," she continued.

Cam turned the palm sander over in his hands, focusing on it. Then he blew out his breath, glancing up at her. "Maybe she did. I can't argue with what you saw, but I think I saw a different side of Kelly. I'm only here out of duty. I'll be leaving as soon as I can." Then his expression grew serious, intent. "You're a loving person, Dodie, and you grew up in a caring, intact family. I knew what that was like because I had that until my mother died. When Kelly and Greg came into the family, things changed. But not for the better. I know I wasn't the easiest son...but I didn't deserve..." He pressed his lips together then set the palm sander with the other tools Dodie would be taking. "There's a bunch of chisels here and a few other things you might be interested in," he said, his voice even, but still holding an edge of anger.

And that was that.

Dodie fought a beat of disappointment. She had so hoped to make Cam see things from Kelly's perspective. Had hoped to bring harmony between the two of them. She knew that was what Kelly wanted. While she wanted to understand what he said, she knew, from the set expression of his face, that for now, she had to leave it alone.

She recognized that look. She had seen it when he broke up with her before he left Millars Crossing.

Pulling in a steadying breath, she played along, keeping her tone light and conversational. "Those look like cabinet making tools. Why would your father have them?"

"Dad was dabbling in making furniture," Cam said, his voice quiet. He gave Dodie a quick smile, accepting her vague truce. "He made me a cupboard that I'm sure is still in my bedroom. I'll take that too, but again, I need to store it somewhere."

"You're more than welcome to store what you want to keep at the shop at my place." Dodie felt she owed him at least that, wondering at how the inheritance was set up. She never felt it was her right to ask.

She knew, however, that Kelly was hoping to purchase a small house in Millars Crossing with the proceeds of the sale of the farm. She also hoped to give some of what was left over to Dodie as Greg's widow.

While she was sad about the farm being sold, it seemed Cam wasn't interested, and she certainly couldn't run it.

"So just take out what you want," Cam said. "Most of this did belong to my father, so I don't feel like I have to run this past Kelly."

Dodie nodded, steeling herself against the tension in his voice.

They sorted through the last of the tools, setting the ones aside that Cam wanted and the ones that were going to Dodie's place.

"You're looking a little confused," Cam said.

"I feel a little funny about going through this stuff and just taking things. I'm not sure if Kelly wanted to sell them or not."

No sooner had she spoken than she wished she had been more circumspect.

"Doesn't matter," Cam said. "I think, after all the time I

put into this place, I should be allowed to claim some of my father's items without asking her. And I'm taking my old saddle as well as my father's."

The edge in his voice warned her not to say anything more about Kelly.

Cam pushed himself to his feet, bent over, and picked up one side of the toolbox. "Do you mind giving me a hand? It's heavy."

She grabbed the other handle and together they shuffled out to his truck. With a grunt, she lifted it so that it rested on the tailgate. Cam jumped up and moved it to the front of the bed, then jumped down and walked back to get the tools she would be taking.

Once they had that and the saddles and tack loaded as well, Cam looked over at her. Leaning one elbow on the bed of the truck, holding her eyes.

"You don't seem happy about this. If you want, I can talk to Kelly about the things you're taking."

Dodie shook her head. "No need. I'm a big girl. I can take care of myself."

"Good enough. Now that we've gotten tools, let's get the rest of this barn sorted out."

Dodie was surprised at the amount of stuff they uncovered piled against the walls of the barn. Rakes, shovels, and other gardening implements. Three wheelbarrows and a rusted-out rototiller she wished she'd known about. She could have fixed it up and used it instead of buying a new one. Boxes and boxes of canning jars and some canning equipment.

She didn't think any of it would get big dollars at the auction, but she dutifully sorted them the way Cam suggested.

Cleaning all this out had revealed a door to another

room. In this they unearthed a drill press Cam encouraged her to take as well as some finishing hammers and buckets and buckets of nails. Boards and pieces of plywood. Hardware for doors and cabinets and, surprisingly, some finished projects. A small box with perfectly formed dovetail joints. A shelf with intricately carved supports. What looked like a hope chest with a tree inlaid in wood on the top. She tried to lift the lid, but it slid off the top side. It was unfinished.

"Did your father make all this?" Dodie asked, replacing the lid, brushing the dust off the top to see the design better. "This is incredible craftsmanship."

"We made that hope chest together when I was ten," he said. "But when he married Kelly, he...he got busy on the farm. We never finished the project. I'd like to keep that as well."

"Of course," Dodie said once again feeling foolish for making it sound like she was giving him permission.

Two hours later they had finished in both of the rooms. Some of the stuff lay outside in a pile to be picked up later and taken to the landfill. The rest was piled up neatly in the middle of the barn.

She and Cam had loaded the drill press on her truck to take to her home.

He brushed the dust off his pants when he was done and glanced at the house. "I know you wanted to get a lot of this yard stuff out of the way, but I wonder if we shouldn't start on the house before we go through the rest of the yard. Get it ready for when Kelly comes back?"

Dodie glanced at the house, feeling a curious pang. "We'll have to go through it Monday, for sure. The OT from the hospital came and had a look on Friday and gave me a list of things I need to do before she comes home. One of which is move a bed downstairs for her."

"I can help you with that on Monday. There're two single beds up there for sure. Mine and Greg's. Unless Kelly got rid of them."

"I doubt it. She told me she hasn't been able to go into Greg's room since he died." Dodie felt another faint pain at the thought. "She asked me if I wanted to but I haven't been interested either. So I'm pretty sure both rooms are undisturbed."

"Good to know. I might want to take a few things from my room as well." Cam gave her a careful smile. "If that's okay."

"Of course. Why do you feel you need to ask?"

"I don't want to make her any more upset than she already is."

"She's still grieving." Dodie felt she had to defend her mother-in-law. Kelly had often bemoaned the fact that Cam didn't come. How much she wished she could see him.

Dodie felt badly for her but part of her was glad not to have to face Cam. Despite her happy years with Greg, she still struggled with frustration and sorrow over Cam's breakup with her.

A struggle which could draw her mind to places she struggled to block off. Emotions that created tremors of guilt.

"Maybe." Then he pulled in a sigh. "She's not the only one though."

And in that moment Dodie realized she had been selfish in her own grief and confused emotions. She looked at him, caught the sorrow in the lines around his mouth, the frown creasing his brow.

Of course he would be grieving his brother too.

"I don't know about you, but I think we should quit for the day," Cam said, his words stopping her from reaching out to him in sympathy.

"Sure. Sounds good," she returned, swallowing down her emotions.

"Let's take the stuff to your place and then I can be out of your hair."

Dodie gave him a forced smile. "I'm glad you came to help," she said. "I was feeling kinda lost."

"And yet you didn't think you needed my help."

Dodie bit her lip. "Well, I guess I was wrong," she said, choosing to go with a joking tone. The laugh was on her. Little did he know.

She wasn't about to tell him the real reason she hadn't wanted his help. Not when he was making plans to leave once he was done here.

⁂

CAM GRUNTED as they set the toolbox on the floor of the woodworking shop beside the drill press.

He straightened and looked around. The shop was much larger than he had imagined. It hadn't been here when he was still on the farm. Greg must have added it later.

The cabin Dodie and Greg had lived in had always been there, however he saw they had added onto it.

He remembered when his father bought this acreage and the land it was subdivided off of. He was maybe eight years old. They had talked about spending weekends here—he and his mom and dad. Going out on the lake and fishing. But then his mother died and life on the farm took over.

Then his father married Kelly, and the only time Cam came here was on his own.

"Where are you right now?" Dodie asked.

Cam pulled his attention back to her and gave her a wry smile. "I was just thinking of when my dad bought this acreage."

"Was this cabin here already?" Dodie asked.

Cam nodded. "It belonged to some guy who wanted to move back to the land and be self-sufficient. Live off the grid. But he found out the hard way that you still need some cold, hard cash to make it in this world. So he sold it to my dad."

"Tell me about it," Dodie said with a chuckle. "When I found the garden here and the greenhouse, I was all excited. I had visions myself of trying to simplify our lifestyle. But it seemed silly to be working the garden with that teeny rototiller and hoeing and planting by hand, when, just on the other side of the trees, Greg was pulling thirty-foot implements with a great big four-wheel-drive tractor." She chuckled at the thought.

Cam laughed as well. "I get the irony. I remember my dad trying to work up our garden with the big tractor to avoid using the rototiller. Almost took down the trees my mother had planted around it."

"I can't imagine she would have been too happy about that. Greg had offered to do the same, but I nixed that." She chuckled.

"I remember coming here with you," he said. He had hoped the words would just be a casual recitation of their joint history, but the shuttered look on her face told him differently. Clearly, he had ventured into unwelcome territory with her. Or at least territory she didn't want to return to.

Not that he blamed her. Too many times when he was by himself and feeling particularly lonely, his thoughts would drift back to her. Wonder what she was doing. Whether she lived here as she had always said she wanted to. Whether she and Greg had any kids by now.

Whether Greg cared for her as much as Cam wanted to.

"That was many years ago," she said, her voice cool.

But he wasn't ready to go back to the quiet and lonely AirBnB yet. Angie was a gracious hostess, but also rather snoopy. She remembered him from when he was younger and wanted to "chat" each time he came back when all he wanted to do was be alone and fool around with the new songs slipping through his head.

"So you've got quite the little workshop here," he said, stalling. "What have you been working on?"

She shrugged, then, thankfully, played along with his stonewalling.

"Mostly canoes. I've gotten a bulk order in from a boating club in Calgary."

Her answer created a tiny lift of his heart. They had worked on her first canoe together. When he found out she wanted to try, he googled and took books out of the library and together they figured out how to build it at her parent's place. Much to her mother's chagrin.

He walked over to a mold that held a half-finished canoe. He ran his hands over the strips and smiled. "That's pretty fine workmanship." He walked around it, examining it from a few more angles, then nodded his approval. "You've learned a lot since..." He let the sentence trail off, guessing she didn't want to make another trip down memory lane with him. "Did Greg work with you?"

Dodie shook her head. "Greg only came in here once in a while. He was too busy with farm work. Sometimes, in the winter, he would come and sit and talk to me while I worked. But mostly this was and is my space."

Cam walked over to a finished canoe that glistened, shining with its last coat of epoxy. "I'm guessing this is just about done?"

Dodie danced her fingers over the smooth finish. "I just need to put the gunwales on."

"So how many of these have you made?" he asked, looking around the shop.

"Over thirty by now."

"And what about that one?" He saw another half-finished canoe in the back of the shop and walked toward it, surprised to see the layer of dust on it. "Is this a reject?"

Dodie didn't answer. Puzzled he looked back at her, surprised to see her biting her lip, as if holding back some emotion.

"Sorry. I didn't mean to insult your work."

She waved away his comment. "That was supposed to be a birthday present for Greg." Her voice trembled, and he felt a wave of regret and sorrow as well.

Though he knew she was grieving the loss of his step-brother, right now he just wanted to go over and hold her close and comfort her.

A line he didn't dare cross.

"You think you'll ever finish it?"

"Someday. It's been hard enough just coming into the shop this past year."

Other than the moment in the receiving line at the funeral, Cam hadn't spoken to Kelly or Dodie since he'd left. But her Uncle Dan had told him Greg had died right here in the shop. So he understood why this would be difficult for her.

He touched the canoe, swallowing down his own knot of sorrow. Despite the distance between him and his step-brother since Greg's marriage to Dodie, at one time they had been close. He missed him.

Cam stepped back from the canoe, trying to gather his own broken emotions. And that's when he saw the guitar hanging on the wall.

He walked over to it and looked back at Dodie. "Can I look at this?"

She shrugged, looking embarrassed. "It's not professional. Just something..." Her voice trailed off and Cam took her comment as permission. He took it down, blew the dust off it, and ran his hands over the body. "Did you make this?" he asked, unable to keep the surprise out of his voice.

Again, a shrug was part of her response. "I wanted to try something other than canoes. Try to challenge myself. And I did. Lots of clamping and sanding and chisel work. This is probably the fourth one I've made."

"And the other three?"

"Are now ashes in the wind."

"That seems a shame."

"You learn by learning and you learn even more by doing. I figure those three were just my apprenticeship."

It didn't have a strap, so Cam lifted his foot onto a nearby sawhorse and strummed it. Of course it was out of tune. But it had a beautiful sound. Rich. Deep.

"What kind of wood did you use for this?" He lifted it, looking inside, curious. It was quite remarkable.

"Alder. It has the best scope of tones. But next time I want to try local poplar. Just to hear the difference."

"How did you learn to do this?" he asked as he tuned the guitar, plucking at the strings, trying to find the right harmony between them.

"I took the course that a musician slash woodworker put on in Calgary." She stopped and Cam glanced over at her, surprised at the smile on her face as his fingers idly picked out a tune.

"What?" he asked. "Do you want me to stop?"

She waved off his question. "No, that's not it. I always enjoyed watching you play."

"I always liked playing for you," he said, the words slipping out. He seemed unable to stop himself from bringing up their joint past.

Dodie's only response was to pull up an old wooden hoop-backed chair and slide it his way. Then dragged another one across the cement floor and sat down across from him.

"Can you play me a song?" she asked.

His heart stuttered at her request. He had so many songs running through his head. Songs he had written for her.

But he didn't think any of them would be appropriate or appreciated. Considering he was sitting with his back to the canoe that the girl in front of him was making for his deceased brother. Considering the sorrow she still had at memories of Greg.

Considering he was the one who walked away from her.

"I'd have to think on that," he hedged.

"What songs will you be singing on your next tour?" She pulled her feet up onto the chair, wrapping her arms around her legs and resting her chin on her knees. The gentle smile on her face tugged up other memories he had struggled for years to suppress. "I'm guessing you could pull those out pretty quickly."

"I would hope so." He plucked out a few notes, finding one of the songs the band had been rehearsing before he came here. He closed his eyes, pulling himself into the proper mind space. The song was, ironically, about working fields that his grandfather had worked. The legacy passed on from generation to generation, tilling land that had been looked at through hopeful eyes, not only planning for the future season but for future generations. An inheritance entrusted by God to be cared for.

The song was written in a minor key, a melancholy tune that expressed the yearning Cam felt for the life he used to have and had never left behind.

Even as he sang the words he knew so well, one corner of his mind played with other ideas, let other thoughts drift around the edges. Memories melded with thoughts and questions.

Could he come back here now that Kelly was selling the farm? Could he even afford it?

Did he want to come back?

And what about Dodie?

He finished the song, the final B minor chord echoing in the workshop, then looked over at the woman he never forgot. She was smiling, her eyes soft. The light from the window behind her lit up her hair, creating a luminescence that slowed his heart, seeped into his soul.

Their eyes met and once again the old connection rose between them. His heart rate shifted upward and awareness sparkled between them.

"Greg would have loved that song," she said finally. "He so loved farming."

The mention of his stepbrother was like a dash of cold water and created a beat of resentment that she brought him up.

What else did you expect?

"I'm sure he would have," Cam said, even as he fought down his frustration. Though he had always seen Greg as his brother, he'd always seen the farm as his and his father's. To have Greg take it over hurt on many levels. But to have Greg marry the only girl he'd ever loved hurt even more.

Don't be a dog in the manger. You couldn't give her what she wanted then.

Could he now?

His finger still plucked the strings, creating an introspective counterpoint to the moment.

"I was always surprised Greg loved farming," Cam said, keeping his brother in the forefront. Reminding himself of where Dodie's affections lay.

"Why do you say that?" Dodie sounded puzzled.

"Greg never enjoyed working on the farm that much when we were younger," Cam said. "When he first moved here, he resented having to do the chores."

Dodie chuckled. "Yeah, he told me that. I remember him saying he was jealous of you and your dad, because you seemed to speak a language he didn't understand."

"I suppose that would be true. He was just a wide-eyed city boy."

"He always admired you and wished he could be more like you. But he learned what he could and was determined to make the farm profitable. We had our struggles, of course." She released a light laugh. "That's farming, after all. The occupation of 'next year' and hope. Greg often said he wished the farm could provide us a better living. He so hoped we would make enough money to afford to build a new house, but we never got approved for a loan. And I didn't care. I love living here."

Cam couldn't stop his own twist of envy at her quiet affirmation of his brother. But something else she said caught his attention.

"What do you mean, never got approved? The land has increased exponentially in value. It made a good income for our family when I was growing up. I can't believe he wouldn't be able to get a loan for a house."

Dodie shrugged. "I don't know what to tell you. Neither Kelly nor I ever got involved with the finances. But I suppose I better step up now that she's selling the place. I know she'll need my help to go through the paperwork she said has been piling up." She picked at a loose thread on the sleeve of her shirt, and Cam noticed how faded and worn it was. She probably wore it because they were sorting the tools, but he remembered the clothes she'd worn at the hospital didn't look much better.

Cam kept plucking out a tune, struggling to square what

he knew about the farm with this. Though he'd been away for seven years, the farmer in him, the part he could never release, paid attention to the weather. Crop prices. Cattle futures. The farm should have done well while he was gone.

What had happened?

CHAPTER FOUR

*D*odie heard a truck coming down the driveway. She suspected it was Cam, but she couldn't help walking to the window of the barn.

The deep blue truck Cam was renting parked beside hers and when he stepped out, rolling the sleeves of his shirt up over his muscular forearms, her breath caught in her throat.

No sooner did her reaction register than she fought it down.

Last night she couldn't sleep. All she could think about was Cam's fingers dancing over the strings of the guitar she had made. The yearning in his velvet voice as he sang about tilling fields called to her in a way she couldn't understand.

Cam's songs always had a way of creeping into the deeper parts of her mind, giving voice to thoughts she couldn't articulate on her own. He used to play more often for her when they were dating. Trying out songs for the band he and his friends had put together. Sons of the Homesteaders.

She pressed her hand to her heart as it skipped while she observed him. He stayed where he was, looking to the fields rolling to the dim blue of the mountains beyond.

What was he thinking? Was he regretting his decisions?

She shook the questions off, knowing she had to move forward.

To what?

The thought caught the lonely parts of her soul whenever she contemplated her future. Wondering where she was headed. She was young yet. Barely thirty. She had time yet. Time to find someone who could give her companionship and love. Someone who would settle here.

And as she looked at Cam, for the tiniest moment she touched on old memories and dreams. Remembered how easy and comfortable it was to be with him. Like they had always known each other which, in a way they had, even though he hadn't paid her any mind until she started dating his stepbrother.

She curled her fingers on the worn fabric of her T-shirt, knowing she should turn away yet unable to take her eyes off him.

Just for this moment, she told herself. Just a small shift back to a time when she felt she couldn't love more than this.

She and Greg had cared deeply for each other; she knew that to the depths of her soul. When he died, she didn't think she could carry on.

And yet, throughout their marriage she always struggled with the guilt that a small piece of her heart was still in the hands of the man who was now striding toward the barn, purpose in his booted steps.

With a flush of her cheeks, she pulled back from the window and took a moment to move to another, harsher, memory. How his deep brown eyes had turned hard, like onyx, when he told her he had to leave. He didn't even ask if she wanted to come along.

Not that she would have, she reminded herself. All she had ever wanted was to settle in Millars Crossing and have a family.

She shook her head at the irony of that thought.

She and Greg had never had children.

But they'd been happy.

"Dodie?" Cam called out as he stepped into the open doorway of the barn, probably blinded by the sudden shift from outside light to the interior.

"Right over here," she said, moving toward him. "I was just...just going over some of the...these boxes." She stopped her halting sentence, realizing how out of breath she sounded.

"You could have waited for me," he said with a frown as he noticed the boxes she'd already gone through.

"I haven't gotten much done." She looked behind her at more boxes piled up against the wall.

"What's in those?"

"Not sure. So far it looks like Christmas decorations and knickknacks. I was going to sort through them."

"I don't think you need to bother. Just label them with what's inside and leave it."

"I thought Kelly might want to keep some of them. For her new place."

"Right. Of course," he said. "I forgot she talked about buying a house in town."

"I think she's looking forward to that."

Cam frowned. "I'm surprised. I thought she would be more upset to leave the farm."

"Now that Greg's gone, she feels lost. He used to visit her often when he was alive." Sometimes a bit too often, Dodie had thought, but she also appreciated his thoughtful attention to his mother.

"Makes sense. They were pretty close."

Again that faint note of condemnation in his voice.

Dodie held his gaze, curious, wanting to ask him more. But their conversation yesterday had shown her the bounds of his willingness to share.

However, as their eyes locked, she couldn't look away. Again that attachment sparked between them.

Cam was the first to break the connection, kneeling down to open one of the boxes at his feet. He picked up an artificial wreath made of nuts and pinecones, weighing it in his hands. "I can't believe Kelly still has this."

"It looks exactly like one my mother used to put up," she said.

Cam chuckled, brushing some dust off. "I'm not surprised. Your mom helped me and Greg make it."

"My mother helped you?" Dodie knew Kelly and her mother were friends. She just couldn't imagine her working with Cam. Even before Kelly, Tilly Westerveld never approved of him. She had worked with Cam in school, where she'd been a volunteer. Always commented on how rowdy he was. What a troublemaker.

Dodie knew he was. Though she had always been fascinated by Cam, part of her was always frightened of him. He seemed to have an air of barely leashed anger about him. Even when they were dating, she glimpsed that anger. Never directed at her, ever. But at injustice. At things he saw were wrong. Part of her admired that, even as it concerned her.

Now, as an adult looking back, she wondered if much of it had to do with the loss of his mother. The changes in his life when Kelly and Greg came.

"She came over with all the supplies and we worked on it

together. I burnt my fingers so many times on the glue gun she put Greg on gluing duty. I was demoted to handing her and Greg the pinecones and nuts and getting rid of glue strings." He smiled at the memory, then his expression grew serious as he set it aside and went through the rest of the box. "I doubt Kelly would want any of this," he said. "I don't even remember her putting up any of these ornaments. But we can ask."

Dodie opened the next box. It was full of gold and red balls. She set it aside as well.

"She might want this," Cam said, holding up a small ceramic house that he had pulled out of another carton. "It's part of a village she always put out at Christmas. At least she did when I was at home."

"Why don't we put what we think she might want in one corner of the barn. We can go over it with her when she comes back home."

"Good plan," Cam said as he dragged another box close. He pulled a jackknife out of his pocket and slit the tape open. Then he smiled as he pulled out a plastic bag. From that he took a piece of cloth with a few colorful strings dangling from it.

Curious what caught his eye, Dodie looked closer.

The cloth was an embroidery of angels, half finished. One angel was completed and just the wings of the other had been stitched.

"Did Kelly do that?" Dodie couldn't remember her doing any kind of handwork, let alone embroidery. Kelly seldom sat still long enough to even read a magazine.

Cam shook his head. "No. My mom did. I remember giving this kit to her as a Christmas present. I was so proud of myself because I found it at Bits and Bobs."

Dodie laughed at what he said. "Oh, wow. I forgot all about that shop."

"It was such a mishmash there. It took a lot of digging to find this."

"I'm sure some of the merchandise was cast-offs from other companies." Dodie shook her head, remembering the stacked shelves and crowded aisles. The woman who owned Bits and Bobs sold sewing supplies, fabric, and notions. But she also stocked wool, embroidery kits, paper for scrapbooking, stickers, and endless buckets of beads in her delightful store. "Going through that store was always like a treasure hunt," Dodie continued with a grin. "I remember Sarah and Janie and I spending hours planning projects from the stuff in that store. I think I even made a leather purse out of an old kit I bought there."

"I remember when the owner sold the store and had a sale. My mom dragged me there to dig through her stuff, hoping to find some craft bargain. I was so bored."

"How could you possibly be bored in that store? It was a treasure trove of possibilities."

"Trust you to find opportunity in chaos," Cam said with a chuckle as their eyes met.

Again.

And again their gazes locked and held.

Look away. He's not for you. He wasn't then, and he isn't now.

"Dodie," Cam whispered, lifting his hand toward her.

She felt her own hand rising, reaching, her breath catching in her throat as her heart skipped its next beat, caught it, and then began thundering as their hands touched, their warmth transferring to each other, the connection now physical.

His callused fingertips caressed her skin.

"Hello, the house, anybody here?"

The rough voice slammed into the moment.

Dodie yanked her hand back and scrambled to her feet, her cheeks burning as she swallowed.

Cam stood as well, looking from Dodie to the man who now stood framed by the doorway.

He wore a large cowboy hat, leather jacket over a protruding belly, crisp new blue jeans cinched and held by a large oval buckle, and cowboy boots that gleamed.

Wannabe cowboy, Dodie thought, brushing her hands on her pants as if to remove the feel of Cam's hand from hers.

"Hey there," the man said, striding toward Cam, his hand outstretched, a gold ring on one pinkie. "Name's Devon Collier of Collier's Auction House. We'll be taking care of the sale. Thought I would stop by and get acquainted. Get a lay of the land, so to speak."

"I'm Cam Morgan, but the person you need to talk to is Dodie Morgan." Cam turned and gestured toward her.

"Your wife?"

"Sister-in-law," Cam said, his tone forced.

"Sorry. My apologies." Devon shook Dodie's hand, grinning at her. "So, Kelly said she would give me an itemized list, but thought I'd offer our services. We can go through everything efficiently, knowing what the buyers might be interested in." Devon's smile got even larger, showing the gap in his teeth.

"That's okay," Dodie said, folding her hands in front of her, still feeling a small tinge of surprise at how Cam had deferred to her. "I prefer to organize it myself. With Cam's help, of course."

Devon glanced back at Cam, as if to verify what Dodie had just said. But Cam said nothing, surprising Dodie once again.

"Are you sure you want to go this route? I know from personal experience many owners have a hard time being dispassionate about their things."

Devon sounded reasonable and what he said made sense, but Kelly had asked her to do this and she would not disappoint her mother-in-law.

"Thanks, but that's fine."

"We could save you a lot of heartache and frustration."

"She said no," Cam said, his smile polite, but Dodie recognized the tone. It was his "don't mess with me" tone. The one that had gotten him into trouble at school and, occasionally, with Gene Sutton, one of the police officers in town.

But it was also a tone that his peers would back away from, and if Devon wanted to keep this job, he would be wise to pay attention as well.

"Of course. I understand. My apologies," Devon said, holding up his hands as if surrendering. He pulled a card out of his jacket and set it on one of the boxes. "But in case you change your mind, here's my card. Not sure if you have a copy yet but won't hurt to keep it handy anyhow."

Cam made no move to pick it up.

Devon gave a sheepish grin. "Okay. So, I'll be visiting Kelly after this to go over some terms of the sale." He glanced back at Cam. "Not sure how involved you are in the process?"

"Just doing the grunt work," Cam said, closing the box he'd just examined and setting it to one side.

"Of course." Devon looked over at Dodie as if wondering at her role, but she shrugged. She only knew what Kelly had told her, that it was her intention to sell the farm.

"Okay then, I'll be addressing my questions to Kelly, I guess. Goodbye and thanks for your time." And with that, he left.

Dodie glanced over at Cam, who was shaking his head.

"What's wrong?" she asked.

"I don't like salesy, smarmy people," he said, frowning as he stood. "Always looking to upsell, looking for the main chance. Acting like they've got your interests at heart when they're just trying to make more money off you."

"I'm guessing you've had your share of dealing with those people?" Dodie asked.

"Too much," Cam said. He shook his head, releasing a laugh. "And, as usual, like my bass guitarist always says, I let him get into my head and park there, rent-free."

Dodie laughed. "Is there room? I thought you always said your brain was too full of songs. That's why you would forget things."

He angled her a quizzical look. "Are you, by chance, referring to the one time I told you I would pick you up after work and I forgot?"

"Maybe. Or the time we were supposed to go on a picnic and you forgot I was riding with you and you ended up there on your own."

"And the worst of it was, you had the food."

"That was the worst?" Dodie flapped her hand at him in a dismissive gesture.

"Probably." He grinned at her and again their shared memories reconnected them. "Anyway, I don't like the attitudes of guys like Devon."

"Duly noted. When I try to sell you a canoe, I won't try the old upsell and see if you want gunwales, seats, or paddles."

"Very funny," Cam said. "Though I think I would love to buy one of your canoes."

"And store it where?" she asked, thinking of the things he wanted to keep that were now sitting in her workshop.

"I might settle down someday. Buy a place."

His words created a pleat of dismay. Why was he able to think of this now? And not when they were dating?

"I thought you couldn't see yourself settling down?" she couldn't help asking. "Not the homebody type."

Cam looked away, and she felt as if she had scored a low blow as she regurgitated the old words he had tossed at her. The reason, he told her, that they shouldn't settle down on the farm. Get married.

"People change," he said. "Life on the road isn't great, no matter how good the accommodations. It's nice to have a place to come back to at the end of a long tour."

She felt bad. "Of course. I get that. I shouldn't have been sarcastic."

His warm smile granted her forgiveness. "It's okay. I guess I know where you're coming from." He moved past her to take another box, but she stopped him with a hand on his arm.

"Again. I'm sorry."

Cam paused, looking down at her hand. Then, to her surprise and shock, he covered it with his, his fingers warm, his fingertips rough and callused.

Then he lifted his gaze, holding hers. She swallowed at the intensity she saw burning in the depths of his dark brown eyes.

"You don't need to be sorry. I'm the one who needs to apologize. I know I have no right to assume that I broke your heart when I left, and it would be arrogant of me to think so. But if I hurt you with what I said, I am truly sorry. Please know that...that I had my reasons."

She sucked in a quick, short breath, trying to slow her racing heart when she couldn't drag her gaze away.

His lips parted, and she had to clench her hands together to keep from reaching up and touching his mouth.

She saw his throat work as he swallowed, then he was the first to drag his gaze away.

"I should...we should get back...back to work," he said, sounding as breathless as she felt.

She stood a moment, looking away, afraid to turn her eyes once again to him. Afraid of how she would react.

She fought down her reaction, guilt battling with the old attraction Cam could still create in her.

You were married to his brother, she reminded herself as she walked across the shop, putting distance between them.

But yet, though they were separated by the yawning space in the building, she was aware of every move he made.

They worked in silence for another ten minutes, and then he announced he had to go. Apologized that he wouldn't be visiting Kelly with her today.

Though his comment disappointed her, part of her was glad she wouldn't be seeing Kelly with Cam beside her. She was afraid she couldn't hide the growing and changing feelings she was wrestling with.

She waved at him, but when he walked out of the building, she made her way to the door, trying to stay out of sight as she watched him leave, an unwelcome yearning whistling through her.

A yearning she could not afford to indulge in. He had broken her heart once. She would be foolish to give it to him again.

CAM PULLED into the parking lot of the church and turned his vehicle off. He waited a moment, looking around, then caught himself.

He was looking for Dodie's truck.

Yesterday, after that moment of connection, he couldn't help noticing every movement she made. He was hyperaware of her. There was more work to do, but he couldn't stick around. Afraid he might do something monumentally stupid.

Like kiss her.

When he wasn't thinking about her, he was dreaming about her. He knew it wasn't a good idea. She was still mourning the loss of his brother. What kind of man takes advantage of a woman when she's in that situation?

He closed his eyes, praying for forgiveness. Praying he could keep his emotions in the correct place.

But once you dated. Once you were close.

You have other plans.

Can't you change them?

The same questions he'd battled all night drifted into his mind again. He had to tamp the tempting thoughts down. The obligations to his band were, right now, his priority. He could dream all he wanted about coming back to Millars Crossing, but that opportunity was gone. At least for the foreseeable future.

But after that?

He stepped out of the truck, his gaze, once again, drifting to the hazy line of the mountains he glimpsed through the buildings in town. They were his anchor. A constant that never changed, never moved. He had missed seeing them, wished he could stay longer so he could go hiking in those mountains. Spend time there like he and Greg used to as children when his father would take them out riding.

He felt a twisting sensation, deep in his chest, memories rising up like bile.

Memories of the betrayal he felt after his father died and the repercussions changed his world.

Forgive. Forgive.

The healing words resonated through his mind as he drew in a slow breath, settling his swirling thoughts.

He had created a successful life for himself. Was pushed into a place he wouldn't have gone otherwise. Music had always been in his soul and to find expression to that had been a gift. To have the songs he wrote in the quiet of his room sung on a stage to thousands of fans, with his band's accompaniment, was a blessing and a triumph he could never have imagined.

And yet was it something he wanted to keep doing? Life on the road was wearing. And though this North American tour was a huge coup, the thought of spending endless evenings on his own, traveling thousands of miles, wore on him.

He put a brake on his thoughts before he descended into self-pity. Reminded himself of the blessings he had and the gifts he'd received. How he could set money aside for the future. After this tour, he could set himself up the way he wanted where he wanted.

Here?

Pump the brakes, he told himself, hardly daring to think of the possibility.

He walked to the church building, smiling at some of the people who said hello. He recognized many of them. Was thankful that here, he was no one special. Of course, he hadn't achieved enough airplay to warrant instant recognition.

"So, Cam, good to see you." Thomas Kennerman clapped him on the shoulder, grinning at him. "How's the music industry treating you?"

"Quite well, actually," Cam said, returning Thomas's smile.

"Heard one of your songs on the radio the other day while I was working the maintainer on the road. Sounded good."

"Thanks for that."

"Someday I might have to ask for your autograph," he joked.

Cam laughed at that as they walked into the church.

64

He greeted a few more people then walked down the aisle, settling into the first open spot he found.

He looked around the church he had attended since he was born. Memories cascaded over themselves as he took in the stained-glass windows, how the light fell on the various members of the congregation. The Geldermans still sat in their usual pew, though they were more stooped than he remembered. More gray in their hair. Hearing aids hooked over their ears. Ahead of them set the Trousdale family. Their youngest was now a tall gangly boy who was bent over, looking like he wanted to be anywhere but here.

Cam chuckled at the sight. Remembered his own reluctance to come to church when he was that age. If it wasn't for the fact that Dodie Westerveld and her family were always in attendance, giving him an opportunity to watch her unobserved, he doubted he would have listened to his father's entreaties to attend as often as he did.

As he thought of her, his eyes drifted over to the Westerveld family pew. Though no one owned or reserved any of the pews in the church, there was an unspoken agreement certain people sat in certain places. In fact, right now, he sat in the same spot he and his dad and his mother had at one time. And then, when Kelly and Greg joined them, they sat here as well.

Now three of them were gone and only he and Kelly remained.

He stood as a worship team came to the front, and as the words flashed across the large screen in the front of the church, he smiled. It was a song he and Sons of the Homesteaders had performed and one he had gotten a license to use. It was a song that spoke of home and community and the strength received from God through them.

But Duane, one of their band members, had balked, saying he couldn't buy into all of this faith stuff. He didn't want to do it. Thankfully, Cam had been backed by the majority of the band. The first few times they performed it, Duane beat out a halfhearted accompaniment until Riley, the lead guitarist, told him to smarten up.

Now Cam tapped out the beat more enthusiastically with his hand on the front of the pew, and as the group started, he joined right in, singing harmony.

The three young girls sitting ahead of him turned, frowning, then covered their mouths to stifle their giggles. Were they laughing at him?

He smiled back at them but carried on, getting drawn into the words of the song.

As it had each time he sang it, the song seeped into his lonely heart and nourished him.

There were so many times when the band was on the road, playing in small towns, driving through endless country, that he yearned for home and a place of his own.

He had enough money set aside to buy something, but nothing had ever caught his eye.

What about the farm?

He held the thought a moment, considering the implications of that, considering what lay ahead of him the next year.

The money he had set aside was enough for a down payment.

He knew that the Sutton family farmed the land presently. He could strike an agreement with them to continue the arrangement. It wouldn't be enough to make mortgage payments, but it would make a huge dent.

He shook his head, pulling himself back to the song, chastising himself for letting other thoughts drift in while he was worshiping. *Later*, he told himself. Later he would try to puzzle this out.

The song was over and, despite his momentary lack of attention, he felt refreshed and nourished.

As he settled in his pew, folding his arms over his chest, crossing his booted feet over each other, his eyes drifted to Dodie. He caught a vague glimpse of her profile, her hair pulled back in a shiny ponytail. Today she wore a bright orange sweater that looked newer than the clothes he'd seen her wearing previously. Her head was tilted to one side as Pastor Simons came up and opened his Bible, looking around the congregation.

"Isaiah 43:18-19 reminds us of this: 'Forget the former things; do not dwell on the past. See, I am doing a new thing.'" He paused a moment, as if to let the verse sink in. "The past, if it has been painful, is hard to dwell on. But sometimes we need to pull up those toxic memories and re-frame them. If not for the sake of the person who hurt us, for our own sake. Those hard memories will always be a part of our stories, but instead of being a burden we constantly stumble over, if we can make peace with them, they can become strength for the future. God makes us a new thing. Redeemed and loved. He knows our weaknesses and loves us despite them."

As the pastor spoke of forgiveness and addressing past grief and pain, Cam had to think of Kelly. Had to think of the resentment he'd carried for so long against her. Not only Kelly, but his father.

He had, as Pastor Simons said, pushed those memories down. Repressed them, but they were always there. And he noticed that especially now that he was back. Seeing Kelly resurrected those old grievances. He couldn't change them, but maybe he could re-frame them. Take what he had learned the past few years and find a way to accept and address them.

He massaged the bridge of his nose as he lowered his head, offering up a quick prayer.

Lord, help me forgive. Help me release my frustration.

He looked over at Dodie again, remembering some things she had said about Kelly. Her relationship with Kelly was far different then his, and he had to give that some credence as well. He had to be careful what he said. Dodie admired her mother-in-law and he had to respect that. Kelly showed a different side of herself to Dodie than she had to him.

Showing different faces to different people, hoping they don't meet. . .

The quote from a song the band sang slipped into his mind.

He thought of the persona that dropped on his shoulders every time he performed. The aw-shucks country boy he presented. Even though he hadn't sat on the tractor for years, he still made it sound like he headed down to the farm every weekend to slop hogs, ride horses, and wrangle cattle. Driving down the country road in his pickup, singing along to country songs as he was on his way to town to pick up feed.

That was him and yet not.

Kelly was probably the same. Maybe Dodie brought out a better aspect to her character.

Cam dragged his attention back to the minister and settled in, letting the words of the service wash over him and nourish him. Let his mind rest in his relationship with his Lord and Savior, a relationship that hadn't failed him. Ever.

The service wound down, and as the notes of the last song resounded through the sanctuary, he turned to leave, joining the groups of people ambling down the aisle.

Again, he greeted a few, smiled at a few more, reconnecting. One woman asked him how the music business was doing. He gave some vague reply and a smile. But no autograph was asked for. Sad. He remembered a verse from the Bible about prophets and hometowns that made him smile. Made him realize that although he may have some small reputation outside of this place, back here, he was just Cam Morgan. The rebellious kid who tossed a rock through the window of a teacher's house. The kid who would skip school and busk on the street corner, much to his father's embarrassment.

As he walked out the doors of the sanctuary and into the large open foyer of the church building, he heard a familiar voice call his name.

With a grin, he turned around as Finn Sutton strode toward him, arms outstretched. They met in a tight man hug, pulling away at the appropriate time, patting each other on the shoulder. Finn shook his head in mock amazement, grinning as he looked Cam up and down.

"Well, well, the down-home country boy has returned home for inspiration for his next musical rendition of life on the farm."

"I might even dedicate this one to you," Cam joked.

"It's about time you did," Finn said. Again he shook his head. "I heard rumors you might come back. What took you so long?"

"This, that, and the next thing. Life. Work. Grief." Cam grew serious and blew out a sigh. Finn, who knew every secret Cam kept tucked away, nodded in understanding.

"We all miss Greg," Finn said. "There's been a lot of sadness in this community this last year. Did you hear that Kyle Gilbert passed away as well?"

Cam frowned, his heart twisting in sympathy for Derek, Finn's brother-in-law and Kyle's brother. "What happened?"

"Turned out he had cancer. There's a whole 'nother story wrapped around that, but I won't bore you with that right now."

"Could be material," Cam said.

Finn shook his head, "No. I don't think so."

Just as they were speaking, a woman came to join them.

Finn's wife, Etta. Tall, slender, copper-colored hair flowing over her shoulders. Cam recognized her from the picture Finn had sent him when they got married. She grinned when she saw Cam.

"Welcome home, Cam," she said, reaching out for his hand. He shook it, surprised to see a splotch of paint on it.

She must've caught his reaction and made a face as she inspected it herself, picking at the orange blob. "Can dress me up, but you can't take me out. No matter how hard I scrub, I can't get the paint off."

"The struggle of this artist is real," Finn teased, dropping an arm over her shoulders.

"No, no... I'm sorry..." Cam felt bad for noticing.

Etta laughed. "No big deal. I'm not that ladylike."

Finn pulled her closer. "But you're the kind of lady I like," he said.

Cam groaned. "You can do better than that."

"Anyway, joking aside, you must know, this is my wife, Etta" Finn said.

"Belated in-person congratulations," Cam said, feeling a flicker of guilt.

"Too bad you couldn't have given them at the wedding," Finn said. Though he was smiling, Cam caught the faint note of condemnation in his friend's voice. Remorse washed over him. He had gotten the invitation forwarded to him, through their manager. Later he received the pictures of Finn and Etta's wedding through the e-mail from Sons of the Homesteaders' website. "We were on the road," Cam said, giving him a rueful smile. "By the time I got the invitation, you were on your honeymoon."

"Well, I guess that's okay," Finn said. "We got your wedding gift though."

Cam had sent them an espresso machine. He knew Finn loved his coffee, though he knew nothing about Etta. She had recently moved to Millars Crossing.

"And it was much appreciated," Etta said. "Such a treat first thing in the morning."

As they talked people drifted past them, a few lifting their hand in greeting. One older man took a moment to say hi personally and pat Cam on the shoulder.

Cam recognized his old Sunday school teacher as he walked away.

"What are you doing for lunch?" Finn asked. "I'm sure the girls would love to hear you croon them some love songs."

Etta elbowed him, shooting him an admonishing frown. "Finn, give the guy a break. He's not on a one-man homecoming tour of Millars Crossing."

Cam chuckled at the joke. "I'd like to, but I'm headed to the hospital to see Kelly. She's getting discharged Wednesday and we need to find out what we need to set the house up."

"We?" Finn asked.

Trust him to pounce on that pronoun. "Kelly's daughter-in-law is helping me."

Finn crooked an eyebrow at him, as if wondering at his choice of words. As if he was talking about a complete stranger as opposed to the girl he had once planned to marry.

Let him wonder, Cam thought. He wasn't getting pulled into some complicated conversation about Dodie. Better to create distance.

"Don't be a stranger," Finn admonished him. "As soon as you can, I want you to come to the homeplace. We could go for a ride."

"Sounds tempting. I'll have to see how things go. Kind of

busy gathering everything up and sorting stuff out for the rest of the week. I still hope to leave next Tuesday."

"Gathering things up? For what?" Finn quirked him a questioning eyebrow.

"Kelly wants to move to town." Cam was surprised that Finn didn't know more. After all, his family rented the land.

"That's interesting. I know she wasn't always so crazy about living on the farm, but I didn't know she was moving. 'Course I imagine that, right now, what with both Greg and your father gone, it's probably not such a happy place for her anyway."

"No, not really."

Then Cam saw Dodie heading out the door. But just as she stepped out, she glanced back. Even though thirty feet and about that many people separated them, their eyes found each other, and he felt a sharp tug in his midsection. He swallowed then dragged his gaze away just in time to catch Finn give him a knowing look.

Cam held his hand up to stop any comment coming from his old friend. "I'll see you around," he said.

Finn got the hint and grabbed his wife's hand. "Looking forward to the fulfillment of that vague promise," he said. "And take me up on my invitation."

Cam nodded and left, forcing himself not to hurry.

He came out to the parking lot just in time to see Dodie's old truck pull away, driving a little faster toward the hospital than she should.

Cam got into his rental truck and followed at a slower pace.

CHAPTER FIVE

*K*elly was sitting in her chair when Dodie arrived, reading a book. She looked up when Dodie came into the room and smiled. "Look at me," she said, gesturing to the chair as Dodie came near. "I'm out of bed."

"That's excellent," Dodie said, brushing a gentle kiss over Kelly's forehead. "And no oxygen." Yesterday, when she visited, Kelly had been sitting up in bed, the oxygen cannula prongs still in her nose. The nurse had said they could take her off but wanted to make sure.

"No. My sat levels are good, which I'm happy about. I didn't want to be on oxygen when I went home."

"Wednesday, right?" Dodie was still uncomfortable with the release date. It seemed soon. Only a few days ago Kelly was lying in bed, weak and on oxygen. But at least the color was back in her face now and her eyes were bright.

Kelly nodded. "Those antibiotics are kicking in." She held up her hand. "See? No more IV."

"Wow. Step by step," Dodie said.

She felt a disturbance in the air, faint, followed by a quiver of awareness. She didn't have to turn around to know that Cam had entered the room.

"Hey, Kelly," he said as he came closer. Once again he brushed a quick kiss over Kelly's cheek, then pulled back. He shoved his hands in the back pockets of his blue jeans, rocking on his booted feet. "Nice to see you sitting up."

"Feels good," she said, holding his gaze, her eyes seeming to ask for something from him. But Cam looked away, his gaze skipping over Dodie as he nodded at her.

"And I guess we need to get the house ready for when you get back on Wednesday," he continued.

"Yes. Tomorrow the OT and home care will come to talk to us about discharge plans," Kelly said, her eyes following him as he walked to the window.

Dodie tried not to let the faint panic circling in her stomach take over while Kelly spoke. She'd put off working on her canoes for a few days already and was feeling the pressure of all the work she needed to get done yet. She had four more to get done, and time was slipping away from her.

And once Kelly was home, she'd need daily help.

"Did they give you an idea of what you'll need to do?" Dodie asked.

"Just that they'll take care of some things. They have the assessment they did when they visited the house on Friday. Then an occupational therapist stopped by yesterday after you left and gave me a list of exercises I need to do." Kelly gestured to the side table.

Dodie walked over and picked up the list. "Looks like they'll be keeping you busy," she said after skimming it.

"The nurse said something about home care coming and an OT stopping to help me with the exercises. I asked her if someone else could help me and she said it was okay as long as she could come the first week to guide you through the steps."

"Guide me?"

"Yes. I assumed...I thought you would help...you told me you would..." Kelly's voice quivered on the last word and Dodie fought down a burst of guilt.

And, to her dismay, a flicker of anger at Kelly's assumption.

"I didn't want strangers traipsing in and out of the house," Kelly continued. "It's been so hard the past while."

Dodie felt a fist of tension tighten her chest as Kelly spoke, as she looked over the schedule that stretched out into the next month. Time she didn't have.

She had assumed she would spend the first three or four days helping Kelly with her daily tasks. The doctor had assured her she would be self-sufficient after that.

So Dodie had contacted her mother to set up a visiting schedule so that Kelly wouldn't be alone too long. Her mother had promised Dodie she would take care of it. Between the OT, home care, and her mother and friends, she'd assumed Kelly's days would be full, requiring only visits in the evening from her.

After her own work was done for the day.

But now?

"I'll have to see how this will work," Dodie said. "I've got those canoes to make."

"Well, that's just a hobby, isn't it?"

Dodie pressed her lips against an angry reply. Kelly and Greg had often spoken this way about her woodworking. Greg often called it a side-hustle, adding a smile to show her that while he didn't see it as a profitable enterprise, he was only too happy to have the money deposited into their bank account.

And now, with the farm not creating any income anymore, it was her living.

"That looks like a busy schedule," Cam said, glancing over Dodie's shoulder. "And a lot for Dodie to take on. Don't you think it would be better to go with the original plan and have a physical therapist come in and help you?"

Kelly shot him a look that surprised Dodie with its intensity. "I think this is between Dodie and me," she snapped.

Cam looked as if he wanted to say something more but nodded, stepping back.

Dodie shot him a grateful smile, thankful for his support and understanding.

"Let me look at this," she said, trying to placate Kelly. "I'll see what I can do."

Kelly gave her a gentle smile. "You are such a wonderful daughter to me," she said. "I am so blessed." She looked past Dodie to Cam. "And I'm sorry I was angry with you. It's just...this is all so...so overwhelming." Her voice wavered, and Dodie felt another rush of sympathy for her.

"Of course it is," she said. "I can see that it's a lot."

Kelly released a gentle sigh. "I know I can count on you."

Her words were spoken gently, but they held a pressure that Dodie wasn't sure how to push back on without seeming unfeeling.

"And now, I'm tired. I'd like to go back to bed," Kelly said.

"I'll call the nurse," Cam said, walking to the doorway.

"No need. Dodie can help me." Kelly looked up at Dodie with an expectant expression.

Stifling her initial frustration, Dodie gave her mother-in-law her arm and helped her back to the bed. She smoothed the blankets around her and then brushed a kiss over her forehead.

"I love you so much," Kelly said, her voice warm. Kind.

"I love you too," Dodie returned.

Then she and Cam left.

As he and Dodie walked down the hall of the hospital, Cam's thoughts piled up on each other.

He had things he wanted to say but wasn't sure how they would be received.

When Kelly so easily dismissed Dodie's work, so easily assumed she could drop whatever she was doing to help, he wanted to intervene.

He recognized the careful manipulation. He'd been on the receiving end of it many times.

Greg isn't feeling well and you're so much better at running the tractor than he is. Yes, it's his turn to feed the cows, but I know you'd want to help.

Your father and I want to take a weekend trip. Surely you can do this for us and put up the hay while we're gone?

Each time he had wanted to protest, but she had framed her request in such a way that he would feel like a heel if he said no.

So he fed the cows, put up the hay, fixed the fences, changed the oil in the tractor, hoping his father would acknowledge his sacrifice. Say something. Anything.

But his father kept quiet and went along with everything Kelly wanted.

Which made him wonder, had Dad been like this with Mom as well?

Because he was younger when his mother was alive, he didn't pay any attention to their relationship. How they got along.

But when Kelly came into their family, he was older and more observant.

And it seemed that while his father could be very firm

with his own son, with Kelly and Greg, he was far more lenient.

"You don't have to do it, you know," Cam said as they stepped out of the hospital into the bright and welcome sunshine. "Help Kelly with her exercises."

"I suppose not, but she is counting on me," she said, giving him a careful smile. "And I know how she is about having strangers in the house."

"That may be, but I still think you need to guard your own time. How will you get those canoes done if you're spending all your time with her?"

Dodie looked away, pressing her lips together, and Cam knew that was a source of concern for her as well.

"They'll get done. I'll just have to work evenings, that's all."

It was on the tip of his tongue to offer to help when he thought of the tickets on his phone. Only five more days and he would be jetting off to Cancun getting some much-needed time to himself.

Take care of yourself. No one else will.

"Make sure Kelly doesn't take advantage of you," he replied. "She has a tendency to do that."

Dodie stopped and turned to him, frowning. "Why do you talk like that about Kelly?"

For a moment he wanted to let it drop. Leave it be. But Dodie's defense of Kelly, taking her side against him, struck the same chord he had just mentally plucked.

"Because it's true," he said, keeping his voice quiet, his tone nonconfrontational.

Dodie crossed her arms, looking like she was ready to go into battle for her mother-in-law. "You know, she's never, ever said anything unkind about you. She's always said how much she admires you. How hard you work. How talented you are."

Cam just stared at Dodie, wondering if they were talking about the same person. "Really? That's interesting."

"Why?"

"Because I never, ever, heard her say anything remotely like that to me. In fact, I never heard anything from her after...after I left."

Dodie's expression grew shuttered at his words. She blinked, then looked up at him, chin up as if challenging him. "She told me she texted you regularly after you...left." Her pause before her last word seemed deliberate. As if underlining what he had done before that.

Delivered those devastating words. Shattered the look of love on her face.

"She told me she tried to stay in touch with you but you didn't reply," Dodie continued. "Greg said the same thing."

Another surprise.

"She did? That's weird, because I got nothing from her even though she knows my number. That's how she got hold of me when she went into the hospital. But I heard nothing from her. Ever."

Now it was Dodie's turn to look confused. "Why are you saying that?"

"Because it's true." He paused, unsure of what to say next. It was obvious she didn't believe him. And that hurt more than he wanted to acknowledge. And if she didn't believe him about that, there was no way she'd believe that Greg told him not to contact him anymore.

"She really cares for you," Dodie said. "I know you don't believe me..." She let her words trail off as she held his gaze, seeming to force him by the dint of her will to get him to understand Kelly's supposed affection for him.

Cam held her gaze and felt, once again, a sense of being pushed aside. Of being misunderstood. He was a big boy now and that shouldn't bother him, but hearing Dodie defend Kelly was harder than he cared to admit.

He wanted to press the point but knew it wouldn't get him anywhere with Dodie. In fact, from the forceful look on her face, he guessed carrying on would only alienate her.

And he wasn't doing that. Not in the short time he had left here.

"Sure, I understand," was his vague response.

Dodie held his gaze a beat longer, as if to make sure he wasn't just putting her off, which he was.

But then a faint smile teased one corner of her mouth and she pulled in a breath, her chin lowering, her belligerence fading away.

"I'm glad. She wants to re-connect with you."

"Of course," he returned. He waited a beat, showing her that he had given her comments some consideration. "So if she's coming home soon, we need to work on the house first, I'm thinking," he said.

"I can come tomorrow morning."

"You sure? I can do it myself. I know you've got work to do."

She waved off his comment. "I'll be fine."

He wasn't so sure about that, judging by the look of tension he saw on her face when Kelly insisted that Dodie could help her, but he had to take her words as true.

"Okay. I'll see you then."

He turned and marched back to his truck and got in. The rest of the day stretched ahead of him, empty and lonely. He shook the feeling off and pulled his phone out of his pocket as he watched Dodie drive away. He dialed Finn's number to see if the previous offer still stood. Of course it did, and a few minutes later he was heading out to the Sutton ranch to connect with his old friend.

And as he drove, he felt the burdens of the morning slip

away as he thought of what Pastor Simons had preached on. Thought of how to deal with the past.

He resisted the urge to put music on, preferring instead to have the window open, the summer breeze flowing through the cab as he watched the familiar country slip past.

This is a good place, he thought again, memories braiding with the present. *A good place to come home to.*

He held the thought a moment, then shook it off, thinking of his previous conversation with Dodie. *Too complicated*, he reminded himself.

Though as he drove, thoughts of the brief moments of connection he and Dodie shared tantalized him.

But right behind that came the memory of the last thing she threw at him, angry tears in her eyes.

I hate you. Never come back.

He pushed the thoughts back, fighting the hurt of it all even as he understood her pain and anger.

He had felt it himself.

Ten minutes later he was turning onto the driveway of the Sutton ranch. Finn had told him to come to the main house. They were gathering there for Sunday family dinner. He'd been warned it was nothing fancy. Soup and buns and cold cuts, but Cam didn't care. Anything was better than eating alone.

As he often did when he made that last turn onto the Sutton ranch, he paused, taking in the large log home, flowerpots now flanking the large door with its leaded sidelights. He took in a large building attached to one of the old hip-roof barns. That was new.

Then he remembered that Carly, the youngest of the Sutton clan, had come home and had built a very popular events center on the property.

And now she was married as well and living on the ranch.

He smiled as more memories of time spent on this place came flooding back.

The Sutton family had their difficulties. Though Wyatt, the eldest, had stayed on the ranch, Reuben, Finn, and Carly had been scattered for a time, but had returned one by one before settling down, making a home here.

Could he do the same?

Cam let the question drift away. He needed to focus on the here and now and not some hypothetical and, probably, impossible dream.

He parked his truck beside the other four vehicles, glancing over at the older house this one had replaced.

Then the door of the house opened and Cam watched as Carly and a tall, dark-haired man came down the stairs. Carly was frowning as she spoke. She looked upset and Cam felt like a voyeur when he saw them stop and the man, her husband Derek, Cam guessed, lifted his hands and let them fall in a gesture of frustration.

Carly folded her arms over her chest, shaking her head. Then she spun away from him, striding toward the house Cam was headed too. Derek watched her, shook his head as he followed her.

Cam held back, not sure he wanted to get in the middle of whatever was going on.

At that moment Carly saw him and slowed, frowning as if she didn't recognize him.

Then she squealed, her apparent anger of a few seconds ago forgotten as she ran toward him. She grabbed him in a tight hug.

"Cam Morgan," she said as she drew back. "Look at you. All handsome and scowly looking."

Cam glanced back at Derek, who was coming toward them. "I'm thinking your husband has the corner on the scowling market," he said, trying to deflate the situation with a joke.

Carly looked back at Derek and waved a hand toward him, as if dismissing him. "He's just annoyed with me right now."

"Um. I can see that."

"Nothing new, right?" Carly joked, tucking her arm through his and pulling him toward her husband. "Derek, you remember Cam Morgan don't you?"

"Of course I do," Derek said. "Up and coming country star of the Sons of the Homesteaders fame. How's life on the road treating you?"

He just shrugged, not sure how to reply.

Carly nudged him with her elbow. "And remember when you're up there accepting the CMA awards to thank your main muse."

"And that would be?"

"Me, of course."

"Can't inspire a love song when you're in the hospital," Derek grumbled, clearly not going along with Carly's chitchat.

"Hospital? How? What?"

Carly waved off Cam's question turning to her husband. "Look, Derek, it's fine. It will all be fine."

Derek didn't look convinced and turned to Cam. "You seem to know my wife well enough. Maybe you can tell her that going horseback riding when she's three months pregnant is a bad idea."

Cam relaxed at Derek's comment, then smiled.

"My mom did it all the time. It's fine," Carly said, frustration tingeing her voice. "I've got another two weeks before it's not recommended. You need to stop googling so much."

"You're pregnant?" Cam asked.

"Yes, I am," Carly said, smoothing her hand over her flat stomach.

"Well then, congratulations."

"And tell Derek to stop fussing," she added.

"No. I won't."

Carly frowned at him. "C'mon, old buddy. You're on my side."

"I'm hungry," he said, avoiding any further involvement in the situation. "And I'm happy for you. And I hope you resolve your...whatever it is."

"Argument," Derek put in, frowning at Carly.

"Sure, whatever," Cam said, pulling Carly along as he headed toward the side door. The one he always went through. The one that led to the kitchen from where he could hear laughter and chatter and the squeal of kids.

"I thought I could count on you," Carly grumbled as she walked alongside him, Derek trailing behind.

"Well I know you can count, It's one, two, three, but what you don't know, is you can't count on me," he said with a grin.

"Oh. That's terrible. Please don't tell me that's a song you perform."

"Headlining on our upcoming tour of North America. Dedicated to one Carly Sutton...sorry." He looked back at Derek, feeling a little foolish that he had forgotten. "Carly Gilbert."

And as he did, another memory jarred. He stopped before the French doors leading into the kitchen and again turned to Derek, his expression growing serious as he recalled what Finn had told him at church.

"Hey, I was sorry to hear about Kyle," he said. "I'm sure that's difficult for you." He wasn't sure what else to say.

Derek gave him a wry smile as Carly slipped her arm out

of his, gave him a gentle smile, then went inside, leaving the two of them alone.

"It has been. It wasn't a surprise. We knew Kyle was dying for some time now. I guess we're thankful we had him as long as we did."

"The Kennermans must be taking it hard." Thomas and Louise had taken Derek and Kyle in when the boys were in their early teens and had raised them as their own.

"Mom's faith is strong, and that's held her through all this. Dad is taking it harder than I thought he would." Derek sighed lightly, then smiled at Cam. "Thanks for that. Not everyone is comfortable talking about it."

"I know it's hard to talk about people we've lost, but I think it's harder when people ignore the loss completely."

"And you would know," Derek said, his voice holding a note of compassion.

They were quiet a moment, as if acknowledging each other's sorrow, then the door in front of them opened again and Carly was waving at them. "Come in guys, the soup is getting cold."

"As if," Derek grumbled. "The girls say that every time and every time I burn my mouth."

Cam chuckled as they entered the dining room. It was a spacious place with a long table set with what looked like dozens of plates. A huge platter of buns sat on one side of the table and one of the women, Cam guessed Wyatt's wife, Adele, brought a massive pot of soup and set it alongside.

"Okay," she said, glancing around then catching a little girl as she tried to wiggle past, "We can sit down to eat."

"But I want to go outside," the little girl wailed, shoving a tangle of hair back from her face.

"So you have told us many times, Maia," Wyatt said, entering the room with Reuben and holding what looked like the twin of the little girl on his hip.

"I'm hungry." A young boy, who looked to be about seven and was the spitting image of Wyatt, sat down at the table. Cam was a bit confused. He'd been gone about seven years, but he didn't remember Wyatt being married then. There was a story there, but for now, Carly had joined him and was hustling him to the table.

The noise level rose as everyone settled in. The twins sat one on each side of Adele, who sat across from Wyatt with the young boy beside him. Then Reuben and his wife, Katrina. Carly, Derek, Finn, and Etta sat on the same side as he did.

It was a vast amount of people, but Cam didn't feel overwhelmed. He had sat many a time at this table. Eaten many a meal here.

It felt like a home.

The kind of home he wanted.

CHAPTER SIX

$\mathcal{W}$yatt lowered his head to pray a blessing on the food, and everyone in the room quieted until silence reigned. Then he began.

"Thank You, Lord, for this food. For Your message this morning. For the gift of community, family, and friends. Help us love and serve each other and You. Help us grant forgiveness where it needs granting, accept it where it needs accepting. Bless us in the rest of this day, Amen."

A moment of silence followed his last word, then it was another burst of noise and chatter as Adele served the soup and Etta handed out the buns. She gave Cam a quick smile as she held the plate out to him. "Welcome to mayhem." She had to raise her voice for him to hear her, but he just grinned.

"I like it," he said, taking a bun which, he suspected, had come from the bakery he knew Adele and her partner ran in Millars Crossing. He had stopped by late one afternoon and was served by a young girl. Everyone else was gone. And so was most of their stuff. But what he had bought was delicious.

"I'm glad you could come." Wyatt rescued a bowl of soup from getting knocked over by the little girls.

"I'm glad Finn invited me," Cam returned.

"So, tell us all about life as a musician." Carly said, grinned across the table at him. "Lots of women throwing themselves at you? Meet anyone famous yet?"

"I glimpsed Toby Keith at a concert," Cam said, not bothering to expand on the fact that he was in the audience, not backstage."

"Wow. That's cool, I guess." Finn gave him a wry look. Cam guessed he knew the joke.

"And where do you get your inspiration?" asked Etta.

"I'm sure it's the same as it is for you. All over. A conversation. An emotion I feel when I talk to people, when I'm driving down country roads."

"Sitting on a horse, overlooking the homeplace as the sun settles in the west," Finn teased, referring to one of Cam's latest songs. "You know, as one does when one is on the road."

Everyone chuckled at that, and Cam joined in.

But yet, even as he did, that same nagging melancholy returned. That sense that he was missing out on something.

And as he looked around the table at his friends and their partners, it wedged even deeper.

"And you haven't met anyone who makes your heart beat a little faster. A muse for your love songs?"

"Goodness, Finn," Reuben chided. "Leave the poor guy alone."

"I don't have to do that. He is alone, near as I can tell."

More chuckles and again Cam joined in. And again, that faint pang.

"Dean has a really neat fact he learned in school this week," Adele said as the laughter wore down.

A clear signal that the conversation was shifting. Dean obliged, telling the gathering about how he found out that hummingbirds don't flap their wings, they spin them in a figure eight. Which led to talk of the birdfeeders Adele wanted Wyatt to build, and from there it splintered to gardening and farming and how the crops were looking.

Cam listened, wondering if they knew Kelly was selling her place. If she had told them about her plans.

But he rejoined the conversation as they talked about stories of the past. Memories. Thankfully no one brought up Dodie's name or their previous relationship, though Cam was sure she was present in at least Finn and Reuben's minds. They were closest in age to him and had even gone on a couple of double dates with him and Dodie.

Lunch wound down and Adele excused herself to put the girls down for a nap, something they heartily protested. Reuben and Katrina said they would clean up, shooing everyone else off to the family room.

Cam got up and was picking up his plate when Katrina told him to leave it.

"Don't argue with her," Finn said as he came around the table to join him. "She's got a way with gardening shears."

"And shovels," Katrina added with a grin.

"Let's sit outside where it's quieter," Finn said, leading him through the French doors to the walled-in garden just outside.

Cam followed and settled on a bench, thankful for the peace. "This is a beautiful garden," he said, looking around with appreciation. He remembered when Finn's mother was alive, how much time she spent here.

"Adele resurrected it and Katrina helped." Finn sat down on a bench across from him, leaning forward, elbows on his knees. He looked serious, and Cam was curious what was on his mind.

"So, you didn't ask me to come out here to get my autograph," Cam joked, leaning back, legs crossed, hands tucked in his pockets.

"No. I have something else to ask. I don't want to feel like I'm putting you on the spot, but I need to know." He paused, biting at one corner of his lip, then held Cam's gaze. "I heard rumors that Kelly is putting the farm up for sale when she moves to town."

So he knew. But as renters, Finn and his brothers shouldn't have had to rely on rumors.

"Yes. It's true." Cam was quiet a moment as Finn seemed to take this in. "I'm guessing from the frustrated look on your face that she said nothing to you?"

"Not a thing." Finn sounded angry, and Cam didn't blame him. "Wyatt and now Reuben and I have been renting that land ever since your father died."

"I can't believe she didn't let you know. She hasn't listed it yet," Cam said, feeling a flicker of unease at what Finn told him. "Maybe she'll tell you soon."

"Do you know when she'll be out of the hospital?"

"I can tell her to call you."

"That'd be great. I appreciate that."

"So is that all you wanted to talk to me about?" Cam asked, giving him a quick grin.

Finn gave him a considering look, his head tilted to one side as if examining him from another angle. "Actually, how are you coping? Being around Dodie?"

"Fine. Just fine."

"Really?"

Cam blew out a sigh. "Yes. Really. She's moved on. She married my brother, and as far as I can see is still grieving his death. My life hasn't changed a whole lot-"

"In terms of..." Finn paused, giving Cam time to finish the sentence.

"In terms of I'm going on a six-month tour of North America. Not as long as the other one I went on just after we broke up, but still. Six months away. You know as much as I do what a homebody Dodie is."

"And she's gotten worse," Finn said. "At least that's what I've heard and seen. You'll see her in town once in a while and then, nothing. Rumor is she's still dealing with losing Greg."

Cam felt a subtle envy slither down his neck. How had his brother produced such devotion in her? What spell had he woven? He remembered Dodie complaining about him. How possessive he could be.

"Maybe, but she's also busy in her woodworking shop. She's making canoes for some club in Calgary."

Finn shot him a curious look. "Didn't you and she make a canoe at one time?"

"Yes. When we were dating. We built it at her parents' place."

"Yikes. That must have been an experience. Her mother is one scary lady."

"Tell me about it. Even worse, she's good friends with Kelly. The two of them are a force you ignore at your peril."

"Peril?"

"I can use big words," Cam returned, smiling at Finn's incredulous expression.

"Peril isn't a big word."

"Okay. Smart words."

"I'll give you that. I can see that the two of them together would be...formidable." Finn grinned at him. "That's a big word."

"Impressive."

"But seriously, I'm surprised you and Dodie lasted as long

as you did considering what you had to deal with. I know Tilly wasn't crazy about you."

Cam didn't want to add that Kelly felt about the same.

"We dated for less than a year," Cam said. "Compared to how long she and Greg dated before that and how long she and Greg were married, that was just a blip in her life."

Finn shook his head. "No. It wasn't a blip. I saw her and Greg together and I saw her and you together. I always thought you two were meant for each other." Finn stopped, as if hoping Cam would carry on.

Cam knew Finn was trying to make him feel better, but all it did was remind him of what he had lost. And what wasn't changing.

"I'll talk to Kelly about the sale of the farm when we move her," Cam said, switching the subject to an easier topic.

"Thanks. We don't need the land, but if it comes up, we certainly want to purchase it." Then Finn paused, shooting him a piercing look. "You should buy it."

Finn's comment settled alongside the vague thoughts Cam had harbored himself the past few days.

He tested it, wondering.

"You're not saying no," Finn prodded.

"I'm not saying anything." Cam gave him a wry look.

"But you're thinking."

"I am. This is home. I can't just brush that away."

"And Dodie is a widow..."

"Of my stepbrother."

"Is that a problem?"

"She's still grieving him. I can't..." He let the sentence trail away, not sure how to voice the concerns that dogged him whenever he was around Dodie. He scratched his head, as if settling his thoughts. "You realize I broke her heart when I left."

Finn was quiet a moment but kept his gaze on him. "I

92

always had a weird feeling about that breakup. We never had a chance to talk about it."

"You were hot and heavy with Helen."

"Thanks for bringing up that painful memory," Finn said. But he was smiling, so Cam knew that mentioning his friend's old fiancée didn't bother him that much. Besides, he and Etta were married, so he seemed a lot more settled. "But we had little chance to talk about why. And I always wondered."

Cam caught his lip between his teeth, struggling again with the grief and shame that accompanied his reasons for breaking up with Dodie.

"I told her I couldn't give her what she wanted."

"She wanted you. What else couldn't you give her?"

"The life she wanted along with me." Cam leaned forward, resting his elbows on his knees, hands folded as he looked down at the paving stones beneath his feet. Thinking of how much time Finn's mother had spent on this place. Thinking of the legacy handed down with this ranch.

"Was it because your father died?" Finn asked. "I know you were tore up about that. And you broke up with her a few months after that."

"No. It was because of what happened after my father died." Cam tapped his thumbs together, sucking in a deep breath. "I've never told anyone because it was too hard to face. But when my dad died, I expected he would take care of Kelly and Greg, of course, but also that he would take care of me. He didn't."

"What do you mean?"

Cam raised his eyes, holding Finn's. "He left everything, the entire farm, to Kelly. I got nothing."

"Nothing?" Finn's mouth dropped open, echoing Cam's surprise and dismay. "At all?"

"I have no idea what my father was thinking. Maybe he

had some notion that Kelly would take care of me, which she didn't. Because about a couple of months after my father's death, I talked to her about the will. Tried to find out what was happening. She told me she had a son to take care of. And she made no secret about her preference for Greg. Then Greg told me to leave it alone. To leave his mother alone. That this was the way it was, and I had to just suck it up. So that left me out of the picture. Even my brother wouldn't stick up for me."

"I can't believe your father would do that." Finn's astonishment made Cam feel better.

"Trust me, I couldn't believe it either. I even took some of the money I had and challenged the will, but it was true." Even after all this time, Cam still felt the cold stone of betrayal in his chest. That his father had done this was bad enough, but that Kelly and Greg had taken advantage of that made it even worse.

"That's horrible."

"Yup." Cam blew out his breath and pushed himself to his feet. "And I don't want to talk about it anymore."

Finn got up and pulled his friend close in a quick hug. "I'm sorry to hear that. I wish...I wish I could fix this."

"Doesn't matter. I have my life laid out. I've got my own income source, and it's done well for me."

"And that's why you don't want to buy the farm?"

Cam released a harsh laugh. "I just can't see myself doing it. Paying for a place I poured so much of myself into only to have it taken away."

Finn was silent a moment, nodding, acknowledging his friend's pain and anger. "I get it. But do you want to see it auctioned off?"

"Won't happen if you guys buy it."

"If," Finn repeated. "If it goes to auction, we might not be able to afford it."

94

"So why are you telling me to buy it?"

"Because maybe you could deal with Kelly before she puts it up for auction."

"I can't see myself making a deal with her. She didn't help me out then, I doubt she'll help me out now."

Finn nodded as if understanding what he was saying.

Cam glanced behind him, feeling suddenly deflated. "I should get going," he said. "I want to stop by the farm and get a few things ready for when Kelly comes back."

Thankfully Finn nodded, seeing Cam's feeble excuse for what it was.

"Thanks for coming," he said. But before Cam left, Finn caught him by the arm. "And thanks for telling me what you did. I don't want to stick my nose in your business, but I think you need to tell Dodie what happened when you broke up with her. I saw how she looked at you at church today. I'm thinking she still has a lot of feelings where you're concerned."

Cam shook his head, hardly daring to entertain what his friend was saying. "What good would it do?" he asked, slicing the air between them as if cutting off his suggestion. "That's all in the past. And, like I said before, I'm in the same situation I was before. Unable to give her what she wants."

When Finn nodded his agreement, Cam felt the tiny flicker of hope he'd been nurturing where Dodie was concerned extinguished.

Even his friend agreed.

"Say goodbye to your family and thank everyone for lunch."

"Will do." Finn gave him a quick smile and Cam turned and left.

CAM SLOWED as he approached the homeplace, looking for Dodie's vehicle. She wasn't parked at the shop and as he made the last turn, he saw her vehicle by the house.

Guess they were working on that today.

Yesterday he had stopped by, mostly because he told Finn he would. He had wandered through the yard, realizing this was the first time he'd been here alone. He found remnants of the old fort he and Greg had made, walked through the old horse pasture, then followed the trail out of the pasture, leading to the hills where he and Greg and Finn would go riding.

Memories assailed him and he had a hard time not feeling, again, that beat of fury at how this was taken away from him.

And braided through that were the comments Finn had made. About telling Dodie what had happened.

Trouble was telling Dodie sounded easy, but despite the passage of time he still felt the shame of a father who had abandoned him so.

And yet...

Cam parked his truck, slammed the door shut, and strode into the house that had been his home all his life. He paused in the entrance, looking left to the family room where he and his dad and brother used to either watch the hockey game or play cards. Kelly often sat in the living room opposite that she had redecorated to her own taste.

Cam remembered having to struggle with the feeling of annoyance when Kelly started fixing up the house, swapping sagging but comfortable leather couches for upholstered stark-looking furniture. It was all clean lines and angles and chrome and white.

Nothing like the comfortable vibe the house used to give off.

He shrugged off the residual resentment. They had transferred the leather couches over to the family room, so at least they were still around.

He listened, wondering where Dodie was.

He heard nothing right away, so he wandered through the family room then the dining room and into the kitchen. This too had been changed. The honey oak cupboards that his grandfather had installed had been replaced with dark wood and granite countertops. When Kelly moved in, she had put her stamp on the place, as if to eradicate as much of his mother as possible.

Cam wasn't sure exactly what he was doing here, just that he felt a sense of wanting to find some type of closure. This was probably his last trip to Millars Crossing. Though it had been the place of his deepest happiness, it had also been the place of his deepest sorrow. The death of his mother, losing his father, and what still caught at the deepest corner of his heart, losing Dodie.

He released a harsh laugh at that thought. He'd never "had" Dodie. For years, while Greg dated her, Cam had kept his feelings to himself, admiring her from afar. Then for that brief moment she was his. And he was hers.

"Hey, guess you found me?"

The woman who had just occupied his thoughts walked into the kitchen.

"I did. Have you gotten much done?"

"No. Just...wandering and remembering," she said.

"I did that yesterday," he said, returning her vague smile. "Stopped by here after I had lunch with the Sutton family."

"I'm sure that was fun," she said. "They're good people."

"And serve good food." Which made him wonder what she'd done yesterday. The thought of her sitting all alone in her cabin bothered him more than he wanted to acknowledge. She wouldn't want his pity though, so he kept his questions to himself.

"So what do we want to do here?" he asked. "If Kelly is coming back, how much do we clean out?"

Dodie blew out a sigh, her fingers working at a button on her shirt. Another day, another plaid shirt for her. Dodie always valued comfort over looks, something he had always admired about her. That and many other things.

"I thought we could go through the kitchen. She told me she was only staying long enough to recuperate, then, hopefully, buy a house in town. So it might not hurt to pack a few things up here." She bit her lip, looking around. "I went through the basement already, but there's nothing there."

"Nothing at all? I believe you, but do you mind if I check?"

"No. Go ahead."

Puzzled, Cam ventured downstairs. The basement held the cold-storage room his mother always kept full of canned food and preserves, a large rec room that once held a pool table, and a couple of bedrooms that were full of boxes holding things from his mother—some old dishes and who knew what else.

But, as Dodie said, it was empty, his footsteps echoing in the space. The pool table was gone. The rooms were empty.

He guessed Kelly had gotten rid of everything. He felt a pang of sorrow at the sight. Though he had no home of his own, he had hoped, at one time, to go through the boxes. See if there was anything of his mother's he might want to keep. Or even his father's.

Guess not.

So he went back upstairs.

Dodie was closing the lid of a box as he came into the kitchen.

"I believed you, but I had to see for myself," he said with a forced smile.

"Sorry. I'm not sure what was all there, but I know after your father died, Kelly cleaned out a lot of stuff."

He waved off her apology.

"So, what's next?" he asked, holding back another flurry of resentment. Reminding himself of what the pastor had preached on.

"I'd like to go through the bedrooms upstairs," Dodie said. "When I talked to the OT, she suggested we move a bed downstairs to the family room. That way Kelly is on one floor for everything. Once she's better and able to navigate stairs, she can move back to her room upstairs until she's ready to move."

"That doesn't sound too complicated," he said, forcing a pleasant tone to his voice.

Dodie gave him an apologetic smile. "This must be hard for you too."

"It's difficult. There is a part of me that always hoped..." He let the sentence fade away, not even sure how he wanted to finish it.

"Always hoped what?" she prompted, holding his gaze.

As he looked into her eyes, Finn's advice came back.

About telling Dodie what happened when he broke up with her. What happened after his father died.

He drew in his breath, wondering what to say. How to start. But as their gazes locked, old feelings surged to the fore. Memories of being with her, holding her hand, being close. He hated the distance between them and took a step toward her, just as she broke the contact, turning away from him, pushing her hair back from her face.

He swallowed a beat of disappointment chased with a dose of reality.

She was Greg's widow and his heart better remember that.

"I haven't done much upstairs," Dodie said, her voice

growing businesslike. "But if you want to go through your bedroom, you're more than welcome."

More than welcome. Which made him sound like he was a visitor in his own home.

They stopped at the top of the stairs, and he glanced to the right, at the room that had been Greg's after his father remarried.

Before Greg came, it was a spare room that his mother used for sewing. Occasionally his mother's sister would come for a visit and she would stay there. Cam had vague memories of an aunt who laughed a lot and who hugged him tightly at his mother's funeral.

She had come a few times after that, but last he heard she was living in Florida. She'd sent the sporadic Christmas card, but after he left, he fell out of touch with her.

Dodie paused in front of the door to Greg's room, as if unsure of what to do.

"Do you want a hand with this?" he asked. Dodie shot him a look over her shoulder and gave a tight nod. "That would be nice."

"Let's get started then." He reached past her, his arm brushing hers as he opened the door. It was just a light touch. But even that small connection ignited a flash of yearning.

He dropped his hand and waited for her to go into the room, then followed behind her.

"I imagine you've gotten most of the personal stuff out of here already," he said as he looked around.

Dodie nodded. "Greg went through it all on his own before we got married. He moved into the cabin and left what he didn't think he needed behind. He told me Kelly didn't want him to take too much. I think she wanted to keep whatever she could. But I never knew she'd held on to so much."

Though Cam knew of Kelly's devotion to her son, even he was surprised when he saw what Kelly had kept.

Most of Greg's books still filled the bookshelves beside his bed. Posters of the bands he loved listening to, that Kelly hated, still hung on the walls. Cam walked farther into the room, noticing the miniature cars Greg loved to collect were still neatly set out on another set of shelves.

"There's more here than I realized," Dodie said, easing out a sigh.

"She kept all his building bricks," Cam said in amazement, bending over to run his hands through one of three boxes brimming with the colorful plastic blocks. "I remember playing with these for hours while Greg played on his Nintendo. I couldn't believe how apathetic he was about them."

"I remember him talking about that," Dodie said, coming to join him. "He got a kick out of the things you used to build."

"So many possibilities." Cam held up a half-finished car, his heart pleating at the sight. Had he made this?

"There's a small fortune worth of bricks there," Dodie said. "I know how much they cost. But they're not worth much if they're just a jumble."

"Sell them on eBay," Cam suggested, getting up to check out the cupboard that his father had built specifically for Greg's toys. Far more than Cam ever had. "And look at all this." He shook his head at the sight. A number of remote-controlled vehicles, game consoles, some obsolete now, complete with games, a couple of old laptops, a garage, fire hall, and police station, complete with figurines and more cars.

Beside him Dodie sighed, as if unsure what to do.

"I can pack all this up," he offered. "I'll see if the local hospital wants some or I'll take them to the thrift store in town after we see what Kelly wants to keep."

"That would be great. I don't feel like going through the hassle of photographing and listing and then trying to sell everything."

He pulled out his phone, opened a note-taking app, and started a to-do list.

"And then there's this," Dodie said as she pulled open the doors of the closet. "Did Kelly keep everything Greg wore?"

"Or some of each," Cam said with a shake of his head as he saw the rows of clothes in varying sizes hanging in the closet. "Greg loved his clothes. I can take care of that too."

Dodie hesitated, then gave him a thankful smile. "That would be great," she said.

"So I guess we should strip the bed," he said.

Dodie nodded, and they got to work.

Two hours later all the clothes had been sorted and the bedding was ready to be taken to the cleaners. The toys had been boxed up, as were the books and clothes. Cam was ready to pitch more than half of what they had kept, but with Dodie watching, he hesitated at being so ruthless.

"Are you okay with all this?" Dodie asked as they taped up the last box. "You must have your own memories?"

Cam looked around the now-empty room and gave her a crooked smile. "I do, and a lot of them were good ones. Greg and I could have fun when-" He stopped pushed the last box toward the rest.

"When, what?"

He looked at her, trying to gauge her mood. Trying to gauge if she would listen with an open mind.

He fought between a need to have her see things from his point of view and the fact that he might influence her relationship with Kelly.

Was it worth it?

No. Probably not.

"I was just going to say that sometimes Greg and I would be playing a game or working on building stuff with the bricks and Kelly would come and help him. Or she and my dad would go to his parent/teacher interviews together. But only my dad went to mine. I got a bit jealous, and that made it hard."

He added a quick smile, hoping she took what he had given her. She nodded, but her look was quizzical. As if she didn't quite believe him.

Didn't matter. He wasn't about to create problems for her and Kelly. Or himself and Dodie. The last thing he wanted was for her to look at him with disbelief. For her to think he was being small-minded and petty.

Besides, it was history. Best leave it there.

Dodie pushed herself off the bed. "I guess we're done here. Let's take this stuff down to the shop for now and then we can go over the other rooms."

"I can take them down. You can start without me, though I'll want to go through my dad's office with you." She nodded and as she walked past him, he caught a whiff of her perfume. The same scent she always wore. A light, lilac scent.

And his heart jumped against his ribs.

The scent he had bought for her when he found out it was her birthday. Greg had asked for his help buying a present. So Cam had bought this perfume and Greg had given it to her. She loved it, she said, proclaiming it her new favorite scent.

Cam shook off any sentimentality attached to the thought that she still wore it. She thought it came from Greg. Another reminder of her devotion to her husband.

Ten minutes later he had all the boxes put on his truck and came back upstairs.

Dodie was in the bathroom cleaning out the cabinets.

"I'm tossing all of this," she said.

"Won't Kelly need it when she comes back?"

"I just checked her ensuite. It's fully stocked yet. But this stuff is ancient." She shook her head as she pulled out two bottles of dried-up shampoo and tossed them in the garbage bag she had in one hand. "I can't believe Kelly left all this stuff here all this time. It's not like anyone ever came over."

"I thought she had a brother?" Cam asked. "Didn't he ever come and visit?"

"Once in a while," Dodie said. "But he stopped coming about five years ago. They had a tremendous fight about something. Kelly would never say what it was, but she did tell me he was no longer welcome. So, that was that."

Cam wasn't about to get into Kelly's family dynamics. He just remembered a gruff man who would pat him on the head and someone who treated him and Greg with equal diffidence. Cam liked him. Uncle Dylan had taught him how to play cribbage and chess and would often challenge him to a tournament with either game.

"Do you need any more help here?" he asked.

"No. I'm just about finished."

"Okay then, I'll go clean up my bedroom, then we can work on the office." He threw the words out casually, but they stuck in his throat. He hadn't been back to the farm since leaving Millars Crossing. At that time he took only what he needed, promising himself he would come back someday to pick up what he had left behind.

At the same time, he felt a lift of anticipation at the thought of going through his old things.

He walked down the hall, past the room his dad used as an office, and opened the door to his bedroom.

And stopped.

It was bare. There was nothing in the room.

He walked farther inside and opened the closet. No old

clothes from his youth hung there. The worn cowboy boots he had saved, a gift from his mother, were gone. As was the hat his father had bought him when they went to the Calgary Stampede. As was the leather jacket he had saved up for months and months to buy.

He was glad he had, at least, taken his two guitars along with him when he left, otherwise, what would Kelly have done with them?

He swallowed his resentment as he closed the closet doors and looked around the room. His cowboy posters were nowhere to be seen, the shelf that had held numerous medals and trophies he had received in his younger rodeo days was empty, as was the bedside table.

He stood a moment, trying to take this all in.

Why had Kelly done this? When he left, everything was still here.

He walked over to the small cupboard beside his bed and yanked open the drawer. Even the Bible he had received from his father when he was ten was gone. The bed was just a bare mattress. The quilt his mother had made him, gone. Cam dropped onto the bed, his hands curling into fists, fighting a very unwelcome and surprising knot of sorrow.

And right behind that, cold, hard, anger.

When had she done this? Right after he left? How long had she waited?

Did she hate him that much? Or was it complete indifference?

He didn't know which was worse. To be the one who created strong emotions in her, or to be someone she could dismiss out of his life.

Then why had she asked him to come?

Right now he didn't have the will or energy to figure that out. He pushed himself off the bed, stalked out of the room, and slammed the door behind him.

Dodie was just coming out of the bathroom and she shot him a surprised look as he paused.

"Surely you can't be done already?" she asked.

"There's nothing to do in there. There's nothing left. Nothing."

He stormed past her and down the stairs, his feet pounding out an angry rhythm.

CHAPTER SEVEN

*D*odie clutched her garbage bag, staring as Cam pounded down the stairs, wincing as he slammed the front door shut behind him.

What did he mean when he said there was nothing left?

She let the bag she held slip to the floor with a clunk then walked down the hall to his room. Curious, she opened the door, looked inside, and her heart shrank.

The bare space taunted her, especially after seeing how much of Greg's possessions Kelly had kept.

She knew Kelly and Cam had not always seen eye to eye. But to do this?

She looked in the closet, pulled open the drawers of a cabinet. She felt like she was snooping but soon realized there was nothing in any of the places to see.

When she married Greg, they didn't come here often. The occasional dinner. Sometimes Dodie would stop by for a cup of tea during spring-planting when Greg would work late. She had never gone into either Greg's or Cam's room.

Now Dodie stood inside the room looking around, fighting to reconcile what she saw with what Kelly had always told her. How she cared for Cam and how hard she had worked to be a mother to him.

She knew Cam wasn't a sentimental man, but to see the stark difference between how Greg's room was treated compared to his had to be difficult.

Is this what a mother would do, she wondered? Completely eradicate the memories of one son while clinging to every bit of the other?

Though Cam and Greg got along well, sometimes he would complain about the preferential treatment Greg got. How his father would excuse his not helping by saying he wasn't a farm boy.

But slowly Greg started working the farm, and after their father died and Cam left, he took over all of it. Hired someone to help him during calving season and spring and fall planting.

When they started dating again, Dodie helped where she could, but she was no farm girl either.

And as Dodie spent more time with Kelly she got to hear bits and pieces of her side of the story. How difficult Cam had been. How rebellious. How he would rebuff her advances so often and in so many ways.

Despite being back with Greg, Dodie still clung to remnants of anger with Cam for breaking her heart. For abandoning her with some lame excuse about not being able to give her what she wanted.

So Kelly's words gave her more reason to dislike Cam and to be angry with him.

But seeing this empty room created a shift. And slowly, as if seeing things through a kaleidoscope, memories, things

Cam said combined with what she was seeing now, coalesced.

Had Kelly really done all she could for Cam? If she was the mother she claimed to be, how could she be so callous with his past? With his memories and mementos.

She had to talk to Kelly. Find out more.

Then her phone pinged and she jumped and glanced down at the screen.

Text message from Cam.

Sorry I took off. I'm annoyed. I'll get Finn or Reuben to help me move the bed later today. Just need to cool off.

She could hardly blame him. Though they weren't her memories that had been cleaned so thoroughly out of her life, she sympathized with him. Her mother still had most of Dodie and her sister, Janie's, baby clothes in a box somewhere. Plus every swimming badge, journal from school, and who knew how many other mementos. Sometimes she would go home and go through a box or two, remembering.

She couldn't imagine what this was like for Cam. To have everything so callously removed. Nothing to remind him of his past.

Her hand hovered over the phone, not sure what to say back.

So she took the cowardly route and sent a thumbs-up.

Then she went to Kelly's room and packed up the bedding they would need and brought it downstairs to the family room.

She brought down a small bedside table and a lamp, pushing one of the large, leather couches aside to make room for the bed. When she was finished she glanced at her phone. Only one o'clock. She should visit with Kelly, but she knew if she went now, all the questions swirling through her mind would spill out.

She wasn't ready to face that.

Besides, if she hurried home now, she could put in a solid eight hours of work on the canoes before she went to bed.

But as she drove home, the image of Cam's disappointed face haunted her.

✥

"So today is the big day," Dr. Page said, his hands strung up in his lab coat as he rocked back and forth on his feet, glancing from Kelly, who was sitting in a wheelchair, ready to leave, to Cam and Dodie. "When you sign out, you'll get some prescriptions for painkillers and another course of antibiotics. I want to stay on top of the infection."

Cam saw him glance at his watch, obviously eager to get off to the next case.

"Has someone from home care come and spoken with you?" he asked, glancing at Cam. As if he was the one responsible for Kelly's care.

"I talked to the health nurse last Friday," Dodie put in, one hand on Kelly's chair, the other clutching the bag holding some of Kelly's personal effects. "We've got a schedule set up for her to come every morning for the first week."

"Good. And a follow-up appointment with me in a week," he added, nodding his approval. "Then, unless you have any more questions..." He let the sentence trail off, looking around the room again.

"I want to thank you for your care," Kelly said. "I appreciate all you've done."

"You're welcome," he said. Though he hadn't been the one to do the actual surgery, he was Kelly's family doctor, Cam understood. He would be overseeing her recovery back in Millars Crossing.

"But we're good," Kelly said, giving Dodie a warm look. "Dodie will take excellent care of me. Of that I'm sure."

Cam caught Dodie's forced smile and sensed she wasn't too happy with the situation.

There wasn't much he could do about it though. The clock was ticking down for him as well. Soon he would fly off to Mexico. While there, he hoped to work on the snatches of songs that had been teasing his mind the past few days.

Being back home had inspired him, angered him, created loss and sorrow.

And had tugged up his old affection and feelings for Dodie.

All good material, he thought, trying to put it into perspective.

"If you need anything, make sure you call," Dr. Page said. "Or talk to the home care nurse. But I'm confident you'll make a full recovery," he said to Kelly, shaking her hand just before he left.

Cam glanced over at Dodie in time to catch her looking at him, a curious look on her face. As if she felt sorry for him.

"Thanks again," Dodie said.

"Well, I'm anxious to get home." Kelly folded her hands over her purse, looking expectantly from Cam to Dodie. "I imagine you have everything in place?"

"We do," Cam said. "We put you in the family room."

She frowned at that. "Not the living room?"

"The family room is closer to the bathroom."

"I can understand that," Kelly grumbled as Dodie caught the handles of the wheelchair and started wheeling her out of the room. "But the living room is decorated so much nicer."

Cam kept his mouth shut but couldn't avoid glancing over at Dodie, who shook her head.

They stopped at the front desk and signed her out, picked up the prescriptions.

Dodie wheeled Kelly outside, and Kelly looked skyward, pulling in a deep breath. "Oh, my goodness, I've missed this," she said. "I'm so thankful to be outside." Then she looked back and up at Dodie. "And I'm so thankful for all your help and that you are here for me. I know I couldn't do this recuperation without your help."

This was greeted with another tight smile.

Cam tried not to read too much into Kelly's comment, but it wasn't hard to catch her expectations of Dodie.

Kelly wasn't the type to come straight out and make demands, but she had a way of making those known with just a few words, a look.

Dodie wheeled Kelly up to the parking lot and stopped at the top, looking toward Cam. "I'm thinking it might be best if you bring Kelly to the farm and I'll pick up the prescriptions," she said. "I've got a whack of stuff in my truck."

Cam wasn't sure he wanted to spend that much time alone with Kelly. Especially after the other day.

Up until now, Dodie had always been around. But he couldn't say no, so he simply nodded.

They got Kelly settled into Cam's truck, Dodie fussing with the seat belt. Kelly made no move to help, as if this was expected. But they buckled her in, Dodie closed the door, and Cam pulled away.

Dodie followed for a bit, then turned off to go downtown.

As they left town, Cam was tempted to turn on the radio. But he wasn't ready to hear Kelly critique his music choices as she always had. So they just drove in silence.

Kelly tapped her fingers on her purse, fidgeting.

"Are you okay?" Cam asked, reaching for the air conditioning. "You hot? Too cold? Are you in pain?"

"No. Not at all. I'm feeling just fine." But she kept tapping her fingers.

Finally she turned to him, her expression serious. "I'm glad we have this chance to be by ourselves," she said. "I need to talk to you about something important." A stretch of silence and more twisting of her hands followed. Cam waited. In some small hopeful corner of his mind he hoped she would apologize for her purging of his room, but he was sure that wasn't even a blip on her radar. Kelly always said she wasn't a sentimental sort. Wasn't one to look back.

Or one to admit a mistake.

"We need to talk about the farm's finances," she said finally.

Cam's heart gave a heavy thud. He had to fight down a sense of hope. Since he spoke to Finn, he had allowed the idea of buying the farm creep into his thoughts. Had hoped that somehow he could appeal to Kelly's kinder side. Explain how much work he had done on the farm. Hoped he could cut a deal with her.

Just wait, he cautioned himself, tamping down his optimism.

"Sure. No problem," he said, trying to keep his voice on an even keel.

"I'll need you to go into the bank and talk to them about... About some letter they sent me six months ago."

Cam frowned. "Six months ago? You haven't talked to them since then?"

Kelly shook her head. "I wasn't sure what I had to do."

"Did you talk to your accountant?"

Another shake of her head. She pressed her lips together as she looked down at her fingers, now twisted around each other. "I did send the bank a note telling them I would take care of it soon. I was procrastinating because I just did not have the energy to deal with it. I was still dealing with the grief of losing my son..." Her voice broke and she looked down, swiping a hand across her eyes.

Cam wanted to reach over to comfort her but doubted it would be welcome. Kelly was never one for any kind of physical affection or connection with him.

When she first came to the farm, he had tried to be a loving son, but the way she held herself when he hugged her, the way she pulled back whenever he tried to connect with her, gave him a quick lesson in keeping his distance with her.

"I'm sure it was a difficult time for you, it probably still is." He still struggled with not only his grief over Greg, but his father. He knew himself how long it took for him to get over that loss.

When he was dating Dodie, she had been caring and understanding, giving him support and comfort that he couldn't get from Kelly, who was grieving the loss of her husband.

"So what happened to the original letter?"

"I threw it away, I think."

Kelly pulled a hanky out of her bag, wiped her nose, folded it up, and pushed it back into her bag. "At any rate, the banker said he still needs to talk to me. But I'm hoping I can write a letter for you to take to them. To say that I'm allowing you to act on my behalf."

"You think that'll be enough?" Cam wasn't sure which question to pose first.

"We can contact my lawyer about it," Kelly said.

"That would probably be a good idea."

Right now, he wished they had all chosen to drive together in one vehicle. It would have been nice to have Dodie's support. Her presence.

Gripping the steering wheel, he cut that thought off. The last few days with her had created a glimmer of their past relationship. Nurtured a glimmer of hope.

But always behind that was the reality of their situation. If anything, it had become more complicated. She was the widow of his brother. He had his plans in place, and other people were depending on him.

114

"Let me know when you talk to him and I'll pick it up," Cam said. "Or I can take you in to get that done."

Kelly waved off his offer. "I'm sure Jason will come down to the farm if we need him to. Or Dodie can take me in." Then she frowned. "Dodie shouldn't know about this. Maybe don't say anything to her."

Cam was curious. Why would she want to keep anything from her daughter-in-law?

He didn't feel like delving into that right now. Once he spoke to the banker, he would have a better idea of what was happening.

"And I'm hoping you can help me find a place in town once I'm more mobile."

Cam knew Kelly wouldn't be mobile enough by the time he was leaving.

It would have to be all on Dodie.

"I don't need to buy a fancy house," she said, apparently misinterpreting his silence. "I just want to be closer to friends and shopping. To walk to a store instead of always having to start up a car."

"I can't do much to help you with that. I'm leaving for Mexico soon." He had to bring it up. Bring her back to reality.

"Oh, that's right. I forgot you'll be on the hop again. And after that your tour. You're a real traveling troubadour."

He tried to smile past the faintly snarky tone in her voice. The dismissive words.

"I enjoy it."

"Well, that's good then, isn't it? Better that you follow your dreams." Kelly turned away, looking out the side window, and Cam guessed that was the end of the conversation.

CHAPTER EIGHT

"*A*re you comfortable?" Dodie asked as she got Kelly settled into bed for the afternoon. As she had yesterday, she'd spent the last hour working with Kelly, going over the exercises the home care nurse had left for her. Kelly was willing and worked hard, but she had a ways to go.

Dodie had hoped that she could sneak away while the nurse was here this morning and get some work done at home.

But again, as she had yesterday, Kelly had clung to her hand, begging her to stay.

Dodie didn't have the energy to push back. Last night, after spending most of the day with Kelly, she had stayed up until two o'clock sanding one of the canoes she had promised would be ready by the end of next week.

But the way things were going, she wouldn't make that deadline. As she had since Kelly's surgery, she had to fight down the panic squeezing her at the thought that she wouldn't be able to fulfill the contract.

"Yes. I'm very comfortable. I can't tell you enough how thankful I am for all you do. I don't know what I would do without you. Greg would be so pleased to see how well you are taking care of me. I know he would be as thankful as I am."

Dodie wanted to protest her comment. While Greg was a loving son, he'd rarely paid much attention to Kelly's needs. And he certainly didn't pay that much attention to what Dodie did for his mother or him. His life flowed along quite easily between his mother and his wife's care.

He would go on his guy trips, knowing Dodie would make sure his mom was okay. When he returned, he always expressed his gratitude, but often with the sense that this was ordinary and expected.

She caught herself, realizing how negative that thought was. Realizing that she shouldn't be thinking that of her husband. His trips were his chance to relax with his buddies. Blow off a bit of steam.

Overall Greg had been caring and loving and he had been there for her when Cam broke her heart.

"I miss him so much," Kelly said, still holding onto Dodie's hand. "I'm sure you do too."

As she looked into her mother-in-law's eyes, unease rolled through Dodie at her own thoughts. Trouble was, she thought of Greg less often and missed him less often.

Now, Kelly's words slapped a load onto her shoulders she wasn't sure she wanted to carry anymore.

"I do, but I'm hoping we can move on," she said, hoping Kelly caught the hint.

Kelly's eyes grew wide at Dodie's words. As if she couldn't imagine doing precisely that. "Well, yes, but Greg was your husband. Surely you are still mourning him. I hope Cam hasn't convinced you otherwise."

The load shifted a little as she thought back to Greg and Cam's rooms upstairs. The pain on Cam's face at the sight of all his possessions gone could still sting. She couldn't stay quiet about it anymore.

"Cam and I cleaned out the upstairs on Monday," she said, trying to keep her tone conversational as she pulled the chair close to the bed. "I was surprised at how much of Greg's stuff was still in his room."

"What did you do with it?" Kelly asked, tightening her grip on Dodie's hand.

"We kept most of it for you to go through."

"But I wanted to keep it all. It's all I have left of Greg. I wanted to give some to you." Again her voice wavered, and Dodie had to remind herself to stay on topic. Remind herself not to get pulled, once again, into Kelly's sorrow. Yes, she felt badly for her mother-in-law, but despite her own grief, Dodie was ready to move on.

That's only because Cam is back.

She pushed aside the pernicious thought, reminding herself that Cam was back, yes, but he was also leaving. Again.

And yet, despite the rational words, she couldn't convince her foolish heart to ignore its erratic beating every time she saw him.

Cam had stopped in yesterday to see how Kelly was doing and chatted with her for a while. He had been attentive, which surprised Dodie, all things considering.

Then he left, going to town on some mission that he had spoken quietly to Kelly about while Dodie was in the kitchen, washing up the dishes from the lunch they had together. It was all very mysterious and hush hush and had stopped the second she came back into the room.

This morning he hadn't come at all. She knew she was being silly, but she had hoped to see him again.

"I took a few things," Dodie said, thinking of the journal she had hoped to read when she had a moment. Curious what Greg might have written. "But, like I said, we didn't throw it all out, but if you move to a smaller place, you'll have to pare some things down anyway."

She tried to sound reasonable. Tried to let her mother-in-law know she was looking out for her.

"It's because of Cam, right?" Kelly asked, anger edging her voice. "That's why you threw Greg's stuff out?"

"Only some of it. The rest we sorted through it for you to look through once you move." She pressed her lips together, praying for patience. "But what I'm wondering is why you kept so many of Greg's things and threw all of Cam's away?"

Kelly held her gaze a moment, then looked away. But Dodie saw her cheeks flush, her eyes narrow. "He left. He wasn't coming back, he told me. What else could I do? It didn't seem like there was any point in hanging on to his stuff. At least Greg was still here, and I thought that someday, when he moved into this house and you had kids, it would be fun for them to see all his old stuff. They would enjoy playing with his old toys. And I thought it was important to make sure I could pass that on."

She paused, lips pressed together, but her last comment struck an old pain in Dodie.

The fact that she and Greg didn't have children.

"And what about Cam's future children?" Dodie asked. "Didn't you think they might want some mementos of his life?"

"He walked away without even looking back. Living his life roaming around the country."

Her words struck a chord with Dodie. The sorrow she felt as, it seemed, Cam carried on without a thought of her.

119

"But now he's back."

Kelly shot her a piercing look, as if trying to attach a meaning to her simple comment. "And how do you feel about that?" she asked. "You're not falling back in love with that wandering man, are you?"

Dodie forced herself to hold Kelly's gaze, fighting her own feelings of disloyalty. But even as that thought formulated, she caught herself. Greg was gone. What did it matter how she felt about Cam?

She pushed herself to her feet. "Do you need a painkiller?" she asked pointedly changing the subject.

"No, but I'd like a drink."

Dodie nodded, then headed to the kitchen.

She took the jug that Kelly used to filter the tap water out of the refrigerator and grabbed a cup. As she was filling it, she looked out the window.

And her heart gave a gentle lift.

Cam had come after all.

She couldn't stop a smile at the sight of him stepping out of the truck and sauntering up the sidewalk in his worn cowboy boots, one hand tucked into his faded and snug blue jeans pocket, the other holding an envelope. Shirtsleeves rolled up over strong forearms, cowboy hat perched on his head.

On the one hand, he looked like the brash Cam she had fallen so in love with. But now he held himself with less swagger and belligerence. More confidence.

Even more appealing than he was before.

Don't go falling in love with him.

Kelly's warning echoed through her mind, and she knew she should look away.

But her foolish heart flipped once, then raced as Cam turned from looking over the farmyard to the house. She doubted he could see her staring at him out the window, but his eyes seemed to zero in on her. And even across this distance, that old spark ignited below her breastbone.

Dodie realized she was still pouring the filtered water into the cup, which was now overflowing. She flushed at how distracted even just seeing Cam could make her.

And, as always, her emotions created that annoying quiver of guilt.

She should be grieving Greg. Goodness knows Kelly wanted to remind her enough of that.

And yet, over the last few days, she'd felt as if a cloud that had been following her the past few years had lifted. She'd glimpsed light and hope.

She mopped up the water and refilled the jug, her hands now shaking. She pulled in a breath as she chided herself. Told herself to settle down.

Cam walked out of her view and then she heard the door open.

She lifted her chin, and turned just as he came into the house.

"Hey there," he said, giving her a cautious smile. "How's it going?"

She smiled at his casual question, nodded in reply, and held up the glass she had just wiped down. "I'm just taking this to Kelly."

"And how is she doing?"

"Good. Just finished her exercises, so she's resting for a bit."

"Okay." He held her gaze, frowning. "Are you okay? You look tired."

"Words to warm a woman's heart," she teased as she walked away from him.

"Well, they're true. I'm not trying to win Man of the Year award here," he returned, following her. "I just want to make sure you're not pushing yourself too hard, what with the work you have to do and taking care of Kelly."

"I am tired," she admitted, moved by his concern for her and for remembering that she did, indeed, have other work to do. Something Kelly seemed to forget. "But I'll push through."

"Seems to me I've heard that before," he said, his comment hearkening back to other times when Dodie had too much work to do and not enough time to accomplish all she needed to get done.

It also created another connection between them.

Kelly opened her eyes as Dodie and Cam came into the room. Dodie didn't miss the faint frown of disapproval that creased her forehead.

"Hey, Kelly," Cam said, his voice holding a note of forced heartiness. "Thought I'd pop by. See how you're doing." He held up the envelope. "Brought some papers we need to go over."

Dodie was puzzled at that, wondering what Cam could have that Kelly needed.

"I'm fine. Glad to have Dodie helping me," Kelly returned, looking up at Dodie, her features transforming into a smile. "She's such a good help and support. And I so appreciate her."

"I'm sure you do," he said. He walked to the other side of the bed and pulled up a chair Dodie had brought in from the living room. He sat down, set the envelope on the table beside the bed, and smiled at her as she took a sip of the water Dodie gave her. "But I thought maybe I could sit with you while Dodie gets a break. I'm sure she has other things she needs to do."

Kelly's frown returned, and Dodie wanted to protest even as she was thankful for his comment. She did, indeed, have many things to do. Plus she was, as Cam had noted, so very tired. She could hardly keep her eyes open, but at the same time, she couldn't seem to still the spiraling panic at the thought of everything she had to get done. Every day she felt as if she were slipping just a little backward with no end in sight.

"I'll stay with you so Dodie can head back to her workshop and finish up those canoes she's working on," Cam said, his tone deliberate.

"Canoes? What canoes?" Kelly turned her puzzled gaze to Dodie.

"I've got a contract for six cedar strip canoes from Calgary Floats, a specialty outdoor store. I've been trying to get them finished. I've got four to go."

"Oh. Well then, I guess you can work on them for a while. Will you be back to make dinner?"

Dodie wasn't sure what to say, fighting a combination of annoyance at Kelly's off-hand manner and frustration with the fact that she seemed to think Dodie was at her beck and call.

"I ran into your mother at the coffee shop this morning," Cam said, giving Dodie a warning shake of his head even as he smiled at her. "She said she wanted to come and visit Kelly, so I asked her if she could come tonight."

Cam turned back to Kelly. "Tilly said she would come and bring dinner. That way Dodie doesn't have to come back here."

This netted another frown from Kelly, but then she nodded. "Okay then. That will be nice."

A flush of relief washed through Dodie at Cam's words. He had gained another afternoon of work for her.

And, even better, for the first time in years, she felt as if someone was watching out for her.

"That will work out just perfect," Dodie said, patting Kelly on the shoulder. "Mom's been saying that she'd like to visit. I'm sure you two will have lots to talk about."

Kelly glanced from Cam to Dodie, pursing her lips. "I'm sure we will."

Dodie said nothing, sensing that she and Cam would be one topic of conversation.

"I need to talk to Kelly for a bit," Cam said, getting up and walking around the bed. "So I'll be sticking around here."

Dodie gave him a quick smile. But just before she walked out the door, she couldn't help a glance over her shoulder.

Just in time to see him watching her, an enigmatic expression on his face.

❦

"So I TALKED to the lawyer yesterday after I left here, and got all the paperwork in place." Cam opened the envelope and handed the papers inside to Kelly. "I just need you to sign this authorization form so I can go to the bank and talk to them about the accounts."

Kelly shifted to a sitting position, took her glasses from the table beside the bed, and slipped them on. She frowned at the paper. "I'm not one hundred percent comfortable with all of it, but I don't have the energy to deal with it."

"Speaking of, where's the original letter the bank sent you?"

"I put it on the desk upstairs in the office."

Other than his stepmother's bedroom, the one room he and Dodie hadn't gone through yet. Unless she took care of it herself.

"Okay. I'll check it over once you've signed these." He pulled a pen out of his pocket and cast around for something to put the paper on. He found a large, coffee-table book of cathedrals in Italy that was lying on the couch and brought it over.

She held the book a moment, looking wistful, her finger

tracing the picture on the front. "I bought this book to inspire your father," she said. "I was hoping we could make a trip there some day."

"Dad wasn't much for travelling," Cam returned.

"I know. I had so many dreams and hopes for our time together. So many plans for things we could do." She sucked in a quick breath and Cam caught the glitter of a tear in the corner of her eye. He felt a glimmer of sympathy for her. Life hadn't turned out the way she had planned, he thought. Divorced and then widowed. Then losing her only child.

"I'm sad for what you lost," he said, covering her hand with his.

She nodded, but then pulled her hand away. Though he wasn't surprised, her reaction to him, her attitude around him, could still sting. And once again he wondered what caused her antagonism. But he wasn't delving into that now.

So he handed Kelly the pen, and she signed the papers with her immaculate script.

"You've always had such beautiful handwriting," he said as he took the pen she handed him, then the papers.

She blinked at that, looking surprised. "You think so?"

"Oh, yeah. I remember watching you write letters, the old-fashioned way with a pen, admiring the curves and even-ness of your writing."

"You would watch me?" Again, that surprise that created an element of puzzlement in him.

"Yeah. Of course. I watched when you baked, when you cooked. You were always such an excellent cook. I know I shouldn't say this, but so much better than my mother was." He gave her a gentle smile as he spoke, hoping, somehow, to bridge this gap between them. A gap that existed from the first fight they had.

That particular skirmish was over him asking Greg to help with the chores. Cam didn't think it was fair that he always had to get up early, not just to gather the eggs but to wash them as well. Kelly had jumped in and told Cam that Greg wasn't used to chickens. That he was allergic.

Greg told him later that this wasn't true, but he wasn't about to disagree with his mother. First off, he didn't enjoy getting up early, so her defense worked for him that way. Secondly, as Cam and his father found out for themselves, when Kelly had an idea, she stuck with it and defended it against all comers and all costs. So if she said Greg was allergic to chickens and wouldn't be helping do that chore, then that was that.

"You think so?" A wisp of a smile teased one corner of her mouth, and she gave him a considering look. "I'm surprised you would say that. You were always so defensive of your mother."

"Well, I was still a dumb kid," he returned, surprised she didn't understand that. "I probably said things I shouldn't have, but in my defense, I was just young and trying to figure things out."

"But you were so angry and difficult," she protested.

"Well, I was probably still grieving the loss of my mother. Trying to figure out how to deal with new people in my life."

Kelly blinked, as if digesting this information, and Cam had to fight down a flurry of frustration. Surely, she could have figured that out?

"So that's why you were so angry at first?"

"I think so."

"And here I thought it was because you hated me."

"You thought that?" Cam couldn't believe he was hearing this for the first time. Not that he and Kelly ever had any heart-to-heart talks. It was as if their relationship stumbled along from one event or crisis to the next. Then along came Dodie, and she became a priority.

That and escaping to his room to write songs for the girl

he couldn't get out of his mind. His brother's girlfriend and the person he cared about from afar for so many years.

"I did."

"I don't know what to say to that," Cam said, sitting back in his chair, arms folded. "But it wasn't true. Yes, I was a moody young man and yes, I got into trouble and yes, I missed my mother, but I never hated you." Struggled with, yes; hated, no.

Again Kelly looked surprised.

"Is that why you had such a hard time with me?" Cam asked, feeling as if a fog that had hung between them was slowly parting.

"Yes. I guess I felt like I had to fight with your mother's memory." She sighed, looking down at her folded hands resting on the papers she had just sighed. "I think your father missed her more than he let on. He talked about her a lot. I think he regretted marrying me. And I know as much as I had a hard time with you, I think he felt the same way about Greg." She went silent a moment, then shot him a quick glance. "I might have taken some of that out on you and overcompensated with Greg. At least that's what Tilly Westerveld has told me."

Part of him didn't want to believe that his father could have subjected Kelly to that, but another part of him had always wondered about his father's and Kelly's relationship. He was old enough to know and compare it to what his father and mother had had. But in typical, adolescent fashion, as long as his needs were met, he paid little attention to the adults.

His biggest beef was the preferential treatment Greg got. And then a small light came on.

"Is that why you were so protective of Greg?"

"Someone had to watch out for him. Your father wanted

him running equipment which he knew nothing about, helping with cows which he also knew nothing about."

"Those he for sure was afraid of," Cam put in.

"Yes. And your father couldn't understand that. He told me that I pampered Greg. And, looking back, maybe I did. But, like I said, I felt like I had to advocate for him. He was just a boy from the city."

As she spoke Cam tried to see things from her perspective. A city girl, rather woman, who was brought to a small farmhouse, dropped into an established community and family, trying to find her way. Perhaps she might have tried a little harder, put more effort into making her home here, bringing Cam into her life as well. But still...

"I'm sorry for what you had to deal with," Cam said, knowing this was an opportunity to mend this relationship. Or, at least, create some connection. His thoughts slipped back to the church service, realizing that maybe this was the answer to his prayer. "I never realized how difficult this must have been for you."

"It wasn't all bad. Your father was a good man." Kelly sighed, smiling. "It's just that he was so handsome, so attentive. I hadn't been treated like that by my first husband. It was such a blessing. And he was a strong Christian, which was also important to me. I didn't want to let him go. I know I might have pursued him a bit too hard, but I wanted to have a home and a father for Greg." She looked over at him. "Then, when Greg so foolishly broke up with Dodie, who came from such a wonderful family, I was angry with him. And then, unfortunately, I was angry with you for picking up what Greg had so casually thrown away."

She made Dodie sound like a possession to be passed back and forth, and he had to tamp his annoyance with her choice of words.

But this is a time for peace, he told himself. A rare chance to create some harmony in this part of his life. Kelly would always be Kelly, but that didn't mean they couldn't find something to unite them.

"But he saw the light after you walked away from her," Kelly said, looking away from him, her finger flicking one corner of the paper. "And they had a good life together. Mostly. Greg had his weaknesses, to be sure, but I think he gave Dodie a good life. And I know she still grieves his death deeply, as I do. They loved each other so much, and he was so good to her. He gave her everything she ever wanted. She was so lucky to have him."

Again, he had to deal with his frustration at her take on their marriage. As if Dodie should be grateful, every day of her life, for what Greg had given her.

"Greg was lucky too," was all he could manage. "Dodie is a wonderful, loving, and giving person."

This netted him a sharp glance from Kelly. As if he had no right to speak this way about her daughter-in-law.

"You still like her, don't you?" she asked, her voice switching from the soft tones as she spoke of her son to the sharp one she often used with him.

He wasn't sure how to respond to this. She was right. He still cared for her. Always had.

"I think you should be careful with her," Kelly continued.

And as he held her narrowed gaze, the warning in her voice annoyed him.

"I have always put Dodie's priorities before mine," he said.

"Even when you left and broke her heart?"

"Especially then."

Kelly looked puzzled, and for a moment Cam was tempted to tell her everything. But what good would that do? It wasn't Kelly's fault that his father had done what he did.

But the question she posed made him realize he had to do what Finn told him and not waste any more time.

He had to tell Dodie the real reason he had left. He owed it to her.

Because as he spoke to Kelly, as he thought of his conversation with Finn, as he spent more and more time with Dodie, one thing was settling into his consciousness.

He didn't want to leave her again.

He wasn't sure how he could swing this. What he would do about the band.

He was willing to try.

But first he had to talk to Dodie.

CAM LEFT THE HOUSE, the envelope with the signed papers clutched in his hand. The envelope that also held the letter that started it all.

It seemed innocuous enough. Just a routine check-in from the accounts manager about the farm business. What created a niggle of concern in him was the comment about adjusting the debt load and a consolidation of said debt load.

He wasn't sure what the bank was talking about. His father had owned the farm free and clear before he died. Cam was involved enough in the farm at that time to know where they were at. They had bought a new tractor just before he left. Purchased a new baler.

But nothing that would require the language in the letter.

He pushed that aside. That was for later.

Right now he had other things on his mind. Dodie being foremost. He was tired of the emotional dance they'd been indulging in since he got back. Maybe he was overreacting. Maybe he was reading more into the situation than he should, but he sensed that the old emotions that had once made him think she was the only woman he ever wanted in his life, the only person who made him feel whole, were real.

And he wanted to, no, *needed* to act on that. But in order to do that, he had to deal with the past.

Fifteen minutes later, he pulled up beside Dodie's truck and turned his engine off.

He sat in the truck a moment, his heart rate climbing as he tried to think through what he was about to do.

And what it might change. Maybe nothing, maybe everything.

He stifled the other questions and his other obligations.

Then, sending up a prayer for wisdom and for the right things to say, for understanding on Dodie's part, he got out of the truck and walked to the house.

But no one answered, so he went to the shop.

The door was open, and he heard country music blaring out of a small speaker sitting on a shelf just inside the door.

He stepped inside just as she put on her face mask and adjusted her goggles. She turned on a palm sander, connected to a hose, and moved it back and forth over a canoe. As the whine of the tool echoed in the shop, Cam watched her. She looked tense and her movements were jerky. As if she wanted to move faster than she was, but knew she had to keep an even pressure on the wood.

He watched, not sure what to do. He didn't want to startle her, so he stayed where he was and waited.

From what he could see she had two canoes already finished, wrapped in plastic to protect them from the sawdust she was now generating. Even under the plastic he could see the gleam of the wood, enhanced by the fiberglass and epoxy to make them waterproof. The strips, varying shades and grain, created the beauty unique to cedar-strip canoes. He couldn't stop a step toward them as he noticed a wood pattern inlaid into the canoe just below the gunwales and above where the waterline would be.

One was a geometric pattern, the other looked like mountains.

They were not only functional canoes, they were incredible works of art. He knew Dodie was talented, but this was a whole new level.

And he wondered what she was getting paid for them.

Dodie shifted and turned off the palm sander, then glanced up and, despite his caution, jumped when she saw him.

Hand to her chest, eyes wide, she almost dropped the sander.

"Goodness, you scared me half to death." The mask muffled her voice, but he heard her fright.

"Well, glad it wasn't all the way to death. That would be awkward to explain." As soon as he spoke, he wished he could smack himself on the face. Such a dumb, graceless thing to say to make a joke.

But to his surprise, he saw her eyes crinkle up behind the goggles. She pulled them and the face mask off and sneezed from the remnants of dust she had created.

"You look busy," he said, glancing around.

"Too busy." She pulled a tissue out of her pocket and wiped her face, looking around her shop with an expression of dismay. "I've got two done, two on molds, and two more to start yet. So I'm thinking I'll have to extend the deadline."

"Which is?"

"In about two weeks."

He felt a flicker of panic on her behalf. He wished he could help her out, but he had his Mexico vacation coming up and then, the tour.

And yet, as he looked around the shop, he remembered how he had helped her with her first canoe, the joy he had in working with her.

How much he enjoyed being around her.

He felt himself tilting toward a shift in his plans, vague ideas swirling through his head.

"You know, I could help you," he said quickly, before he could change his mind.

She frowned at him, tucking the tissue back in her pocket as she lowered her goggles again. "I appreciate the offer, but you're around for like, two more days and then you're off to sun and fun. It would be some help, but not enough."

"I know," he said, moving closer, running his hands over the other canoe she had already laid out on the frame, appreciating how smooth it felt, admiring her craftsmanship. "But I'm thinking, I might cancel the trip."

She stared at him. "Cancel the trip? Really?"

And after that?

He couldn't go too far in that direction. The tour was all set, there was no backing out of it.

Did he dare hope he could create some connection, some relationship with Dodie while he was here?

One day at a time, he reminded himself.

"It's just Mexico. Besides, I get as much inspiration being here as I would being down there. Maybe even more. After all, this is the lifestyle I sing about."

Her smile widened, but then she shook her head, as if having second thoughts. "I can't ask you to do that," she said. "I'm sure you're looking forward to it."

And then he held her gaze, their eyes locking, and he moved closer. The canoe she was working on was between them, but it didn't matter. It was as if the attraction between them buzzed with anticipation. A waiting for something else to happen.

Her hand rested on the wood between them. He covered it with his, squeezed gently. Pulled in a breath he had lost for a moment.

"I want to help," he said, his voice low. "I don't want to see you so stressed. It bothers me."

"But your trip..." Her voice faded, sounding as breathless as he felt.

"Doesn't matter. Not if I can stay here and help you."

She swallowed, then nodded, her fingers tightening their grip on his. "Okay then. I accept."

He wanted to kiss her, but the canoe was between them.

Later, he told himself, fairly sure he didn't imagine the sparks flying between them.

Fairly sure she felt them too.

"So, I'm guessing I can use that palm sander we brought back from the farm?" he asked, rolling down his sleeves, buttoning them up against the dust he expected to generate.

"It works great, but I don't have a hose for it."

"So it will get pretty dusty in here."

"Wear a mask. I have some disposable ones that I use in a pinch."

Prosaic conversation. Ordinary talk. But even as he got himself ready for work, he felt as if something important had shifted between them. An old discomfort now faded away.

And as he put his mask on, he knew his plan to kiss her would have to wait for sure.

CHAPTER NINE

"Just be careful with that resin," Dodie instructed as she handed Cam a pail. Yesterday they had finished sanding the canoe. This afternoon they had laid the fiberglass coating over the canoe and were ready to brush the resin on. This was the tricky part. Though they could roll out any wrinkles that would occur, she still liked to keep things as smooth as possible on the initial application. "This formulation is thicker than the one we used when we made our canoe."

Our canoe. She couldn't help saying that, and she found it didn't matter.

"Speaking of, where is it now?"

"It's at the lake by my place. My dad uses it from time to time. It's tippy, but he's used to it."

Cam gave her a wry look. "He doesn't mind canoeing in something a rabble-rouser like me helped build?"

Dodie smiled. "My father liked you. In fact, he told me

that blending families is always a struggle. His uncle remarried when his cousin was seven and the stepmother brought three girls into the family. They got along well, but my dad said their parents worked hard at it."

Which made Dodie wonder if Kelly and Cam's father did the same. From some comments Cam and, later, Greg had made, it didn't always sound like an ideal situation.

"That would help."

He was quiet, looking pensive, and Dodie wondered if he was thinking of his blended family as he gently brushed the resin onto the canoe. Then he smiled. "I always love how this step brings the colors out even more." Guess that topic was exhausted for now.

"I know. They look so much richer," she said. She knew there were more layers to the story, but also knew when to leave things alone.

"And I have to say, the pieces of wood you worked into the design along the top of the canoe are stunning."

She wanted to tease him about using the word *stunning*, but his compliment distracted her. "You think so? I wasn't sure, but thought it would add some interest."

"It does more than that," he said, smiling as he brushed. "It turns it from an already beautiful canoe into a work of art. I don't know how comfortable I would feel putting a canoe like this into the water."

"I just wanted to try something different," she said, disconcerted to catch his dark eyes holding hers. She knew she should look away. Carry on. But it seemed each time their gazes tangled, another connection drew them together.

Be careful, her mind warned her. He may have canceled his trip to Mexico, but eventually he's still leaving.

"Well, you succeeded," he said. "It's so impressive."

Another flush warmed her cheeks at his praise. She didn't know what to say after that so just brushed, the ensuing silence surprisingly comfortable, broken only by the soft music playing on the speaker she had set up in the workshop.

Then Cam lifted his head, cocking it to one side as if to hear better. "Listen to this idiot," he said, holding up his brush, pointing it to the radio. "Thinks he can actually sing."

Dodie chuckled at his comment as one of his songs flowed into the shop. She had curated this playlist herself and had downloaded a couple of his band's albums.

"I think he's got an incredible voice," she couldn't help saying as her cheeks warmed. "And this is one of my favorite songs."

"Really?" Once again Cam was looking at her, but this time a smile teased his lips.

"'Slinging stones across the lake, counting as they skipped, in time to the beating of your heart, the trembling of your lips.'"

"Wow, that's not corny," Cam said, his smile growing as the song carried on.

"I think it's beautiful. The music makes it so melancholy. Do you write a lot of the songs your band sings?"

"Most of them. It's easier than trying to cover other artist's stuff. That can get pricey unless they're an up-and-coming singer who wants the exposure." He returned to his brushing as Dodie listened to the rest of the song. Distracted as the song talked about driving along the lake, going for swims in the night. How the water washed over them like a caress...

She swallowed as thoughts and memories layered over the song. The very things she and Cam did when they were dating. The one time they went swimming in the dark. It was just like the song.

Then her breath stuttered as memories plucked at her with anxious fingers.

"Is this song about-" She stopped, hardly daring to presume.

"You," he said without hesitation, his eyes still on the resin he was applying. "And so is 'Holding my Heart,' 'Don't like Feelin' This Way', 'Prairie Crocus Lullaby,' and a few others."

She tried to grasp the words that washed over her. Tried to fit the words of the songs she'd sung along to when she was working here in her workshop and Greg was out planting crops, working fields, or working with the cattle. She'd turn the sound up, knowing Greg wouldn't be coming for hours to catch her singing along to ballads about riding the range. He didn't like listening to his brother's songs, and that had gotten worse the past few years.

"I...I don't know what...really?" She stuttered through her question, unable to mesh what the songs said with what he told her .

"Really." His succinct word echoed in the silence after the song was over and Dodie was still trying to put this all together.

"Why?"

He had broken up with her, told her he couldn't give her what she wanted. When she watched him leave, it was as if an invisible cord connecting them stretched tighter and tighter, pulling out pieces of her heart with every step he took away from her.

Then, behind the surprise, shock, and confusion came the anger that inevitably arose whenever she thought of what he had done to her.

"How could you take what we had and write songs about it?" She wanted to toss her paintbrush aside, but once they started on this step, she knew she had to finish it.

Standing right across from the man who could tangle her emotions into such a knot that she never knew where love started and indignation ended. With a lot of confusion mixed in.

"How could you take advantage of what I thought was something so special-" She cut herself off before she made an even larger fool of herself.

They were halfway done and she couldn't slap on the resin fast enough, struggling to be careful not to leave drips. She didn't want to be around him anymore. She'd ask him to leave, but right now she needed his help.

"I didn't take advantage," he said, his voice quiet. Subdued. "I took everything I felt myself, all the emotions I didn't know what to do with, and I poured them into the songs."

"Which emotions?" she snapped, frustration and the old sorrow rising, much to her chagrin. "You walked away from me without a backward glance. Throwing out some excuse about how you couldn't give me what I wanted when what you wanted was to leave. You didn't want to stay. You hid behind that excuse."

Cam's expression grew dark and she thought she might have pushed things too far. Though she had never been the recipient, she knew he had a bad temper. It had gotten him into trouble with her uncle, the principal at school from time to time. She knew it had also been a cause of the friction between him and Kelly.

But he kept brushing, and so did she.

The music coming from the speaker seemed to taunt them as the singer of the next song crooned about faithful love that stands the test of time, passing the finals with flying colors, and various other clichés that country music loved to excavate and twist.

Finally, they were done. Dodie, her heart still pounding with anger, her hands still trembling, took a moment to look it over, satisfied with her side. Then she walked around to his, looking it over. Also good. No wrinkles. Smooth and shiny and perfect.

Cam set the brush in a tub of turpentine Dodie had set on a small table at one end of the canoe but didn't move, staring down at her.

She had to fight the urge to take a step back. Instead she put her brush in the tub as well and, without a word, poured the leftover resin into his container and snapped the lid on it.

"Thanks for your help," was all she could manage.

More silence.

Then he sucked in a deep breath, glancing away, as if he wasn't sure what to do next. "Finn told me I should talk to you," he finally said.

"What about?" This wasn't what she expected him to say.

Another deep breath as he plunged his hands through his hair and turned to her. She hoped he didn't have any resin on his hands, because that would mess up those thick, brown waves.

She shook off the foolish thought, holding Cam's level gaze.

"Can we talk outside?" he asked. "The fumes are getting to me."

They were affecting her too, so she nodded and spun around, striding around the unfinished canoe still on the mold, past the planer, the stack of cedar strips waiting to be planed, and then out the door.

She walked to her favorite and most peaceful place on the yard—the bench tucked into an abundance of flower beds overlooking the garden. She sat down, pulling in a deep breath of fresh air as she looked over the large plot. She had planted the garden while Kelly was in the hospital. Had transplanted her tomato, pepper, and cucumbers in the greenhouse and a few other plants she was experimenting with.

A FAMILY'S PROMISE

Cam sat down beside her, leaning forward, clasping his hands between his knees, looking out, as she did, over the garden.

"You always plant such a big garden?" he asked.

She fought down a beat of annoyance at his evasive comment. She sent up a prayer for patience. She'd been praying a lot more since Cam had come. Praying about her feelings, praying about the guilt she had carried ever since she married Greg.

But she played along, waiting to see where he would go.

"I pretty much always have," she said. "I always wanted to be as self-sufficient as I can. I enjoy knowing where my vegetables come from. Besides, I love trying different varieties."

"And the greenhouse?"

She leaned back against the bench, crossing her arms. "That's my favorite project. It took me a couple of years to get someone willing to build it to my specs."

"Greg didn't put it together for you?"

"No. He could never understand my love of growing things and experimentation. He always said the grocery store wasn't far. Why would I want to go through all that work? And we won't even talk about all the flowers."

She glanced over at the house, letting herself relax, smiling at the peonies with their thick, fat heads nodding in the faint breeze, shedding petals. She had an enormous bouquet of them already cut in the house. The scent was incredible.

"Sure got lots of those going as well," Cam said.

"I love planting. I love working in the dirt, the expectation, waiting for things to come up. I think each year I've been here I've added something to the flower garden. Or figured on other vegetables I want to grow. I've a plan for the next five years."

141

"That's some dedication," Cam said with a smile. "I knew you enjoyed growing things, I just never saw the result."

"That's why I love this place so much," Dodie said. She smiled as she looked around at the results of her work. Though she never got much help from Greg, she was always thankful that he put up with her obsession. "I feel settled here. I feel at peace here. Despite what happened, this is my home."

"What you mean, despite what happened?"

Dodie looked down, testing her feelings, wondering if she could talk about it. Then she looked over at Cam in time to see his eyes holding hers, and she remembered how sympathetic he could be. How gentle.

"Finding Greg's body in the shop." It surprised her that she could say that with little emotion. Her voice didn't waver, and the usual tears didn't come.

Cam moved closer, and took her hand between his, stroking it.

"That must've been so difficult."

She let her thoughts sift back to that time and gave him a soft smile. "It used to hurt way more. I remember the pastor telling me that someday the memories would bring a smile instead of pain. He was right. I'm thankful for the time Greg and I had together, but it's easier to think about him and not be sad."

"I'm glad to hear that," Cam said. "I'm glad for your sake and for..."

Dodie waited for him to finish his sentence, but he just looked down at their joined hands, his thumb moving lightly over the back of hers.

Her heart trembled at his touch. It was just a simple contact, but she couldn't stop the feelings it generated.

Nor could she let his sentence hang between them. "For my sake and for what?"

Another beat of silence, his thumb still caressing her hand.

"What were you gonna say?" she pressed. She felt as if she was trembling on the precipice of some emotion she couldn't name but was tangled in the man beside her. All her married life she had fought thoughts of him. Though she had been faithful to Greg, there was always one corner of her mind that wondered about Cam. That missed him.

Cam blinked, as if contemplating his answer, then lifted his head. "For your sake and for mine. That's what I was going to say. I'm glad you're able to move on. I know Greg was important to you." He bit his lip. Then looked away.

"He was important to me," Dodie said, words pushing at the back of her throat, struggling to be released. Words she had held back so long, and now, as a man she had never stopped loving was holding her hand and stroking it, they spilled out. "But I never forgot you. Never."

His sharp inhale of breath showed her how her words affected him. His hand tightening on hers, how his eyes drilled into her. "I never forgot you either."

And then the questions that had haunted her all these years came tumbling out. "Then why did you leave me? Why did you tell me you couldn't give me what I wanted and then just walk away? You took a part of my heart with you when you did that." And now, as she spoke, her voice quivered with emotion. She blinked back tears, and with those tears the guilt returned.

The guilt that the memory of losing Cam all those years ago hurt as much, if not more, than Greg's death.

Cam closed his eyes, as if weighing his next words.

"And this is what I wanted to talk to you about," he said finally. "The reason I walked away from you. The reason I broke up with you." He bit his lip again, as if he still wasn't sure of what he had to say, and then he pulled his hands back, creating a distance between them.

"I know you've always loved being settled," he said, his voice strained. "Staying in one place. I know how much you love Millars Crossing. You have so many connections here. Your sister and her kids, your mother and father, your aunts and uncles, all your cousins." He released a harsh laugh. "There were so many times I was jealous of all the family you have here."

"But you were born and raised here too. Your grandfather farmed the same place that you did." The place that Kelly was now putting up for sale. The thought created a hitch in her heart.

Cam nodded, then tweaked out a wry smile. "I know I have a rich legacy, and I know there was a part of me that was thrilled when dad got remarried and I would have a brother. And a mother. I just didn't think..." He shook his head, as if still trying to understand something. "I just didn't think my dad would forget about me."

"What do you mean? You and your dad were so close. I remember Greg being jealous of your relationship. You two were always working together."

"We were, and we were close. Somehow, I don't know how or why it happened, but something changed between us." He paused. "The last year, before he died, Kelly pushed Greg to get more involved in the farm. Pushed my dad to let him do more, To my surprise, Greg was okay with it. After he broke up with you, he started helping more. Dad even talked about Greg and me being future partners. It was a good time. I started making plans for you and me." He stopped, and Dodie had to fight down her questions, knowing she had to let him find his own way through the story. "But then things started getting tense. Dad started retreating from me. He and Kelly grew closer and started keeping me out of the loop. And then, when he died, he left everything to Kelly."

Dodie frowned. "What you mean 'everything'?"

"Pretty straightforward. Everything. In his will he stated the farm was to go to her. All the equipment, machinery, livestock. Everything. He changed it about six months before he died."

"He didn't know he was going to die though?"

"No. That was unexpected. Though I have to confess, I talked to his lawyer. I was so angry and upset and hurting. I was looking for a reason for this happening. Anything."

It wasn't hard to hear the bitter tone in his voice. Dodie didn't blame him. She couldn't imagine why his father would have done that.

"But you kept working on the farm," Dodie said, still feeling confused. "And I know you loved it. It was one of the big things we had in common. A love for the land and working it. Growing things."

Cam released a harsh laugh. "Of course I kept working it. It was all I could do. I had the band, but that was always just a side hustle. I didn't think singing would become what it has."

"You didn't think you'd be this successful?" She was still puzzled.

"I didn't think I'd *have* to be this successful. Farming was the one thing I wanted to do more than anything. I just happen to love writing songs and performing as well, but it was a lot of work and time and hustle, hustle to get to where we are now. And even now, it's still a tough gig. I've set aside some money, but only because I've been living off sandwiches and protein bars."

"So then why did you walk away from it all? You and Greg could still have been partners on the farm." She frowned, still scrambling to put everything together.

Cam pressed his lips together as if trying to make a decision.

Then he turned to her, his eyes holding hers, his gaze intent. "I know you and Kelly get along well, but I'm hoping you can understand my side of the story. Why I did what I did all those years ago. Once I got over the initial shock of Dad's death, Kelly and I sat down together to go over what we would do with the farm. Or rather, what she would do with the farm. She made it very clear that there was no room for me. That the farm was hers, and she was making Greg her partner. I would have no part of it. I doubt that was Dad's intent when he willed it all to Kelly, but there was nothing I could do about it."

Dodie's heart thundered in her chest as the impact of what he said dropped into her soul. A week ago she might have thought he was being dramatic. Not telling the truth.

She thought of Cam's empty room, everything stripped out of it. As if Kelly was trying to extinguish him from her memory and her life when he left.

"How could she have done that? I can't believe she would have." As soon as she spoke, she wanted to take the words back. She didn't want him to think she doubted his story.

"I know. And that's why I said nothing to you. Not about Kelly anyway. But after Kelly spoke to me and laid things out pretty black and white, I knew there was no future for me on the farm. Which meant I couldn't give you what you wanted. A life, here in Millars Crossing, growing things and raising kids, living on the farm. I had to leave. I couldn't stay here and watch the farm I had worked since my first memory being taken care of by someone who didn't value it the same way I did."

Dodie sat back, sorting through what he said. And slowly, she understood the why of his actions.

"And so you left."

He nodded, his eyes still holding hers. "Would you have come with me?"

And to her shame, she couldn't immediately say yes. Say without hesitation that she would have followed him to the ends of the earth. Because the truth was, at that time, she had never wanted to leave Millars Crossing. He was right about that.

"I sensed that," he continued, correctly interpreting her hesitation. "And I loved you too much to take away what I know you wanted. To make you choose. I didn't want you coming with me and living a ragged life and regretting that choice. Missing home, lonely, starting over somewhere else with virtually nothing. Because the only thing I had after I drove away from here was my truck and two guitars. That's it. I had nothing more to offer you. I know how you grew up, You have never wanted for anything. And I know you're not a spoiled brat, I know possessions don't mean that much to you, but I also know that home and family did and still do. And I couldn't give you that. I figured it was easy just to make a break and leave you behind for your own sake."

"And break my heart in the process," Dodie said quietly. She gave him a careful smile. "Trouble is, you know me all too well." And listening to him, looking at her life through his eyes, she felt a flush of shame.

"At the same time," she continued, "I wish you would've told me. I wish you would've let me choose."

"Maybe I didn't give you enough credit," Cam said. "But I had my own idea of the life I wanted to live with you. And trust me, the life I lived when I left here was not one I would have wanted to share with you. Looking back, I made the right decision."

"But you had no choice either," she said.

"I know. Kelly didn't even offer me a job as a hired hand on the farm."

Dodie pressed her fingers to her forehead, her thoughts battling each other. She and Kelly had always enjoyed each other's company. Kelly had been unfailingly generous with her. She couldn't mesh what Cam told her with the woman she knew.

"You look like you doubt me," Cam ground out.

Wasn't hard to hear the anger in his voice and also the disappointment.

"You have to understand. This is a tremendous shift for me in how I see someone I get along well with."

Cam held her gaze, then lifted his hand in a gesture of peace. "I understand that. But you have to add to the mix that you were married to Greg. Her dearly beloved biological son."

Dodie waited, trying to find the right words to parse her thoughts. To put what he had just told her in perspective with that empty room. The way Kelly would talk about Cam.

Much as she hated to admit it, there were many times she had gone along with Kelly's disparaging remarks. Her mother-in-law's negative words stoked the pain and anger she felt when Cam drove out of her yard and her life, watching him through tear-filled eyes, not understanding what had happened. For a long time she thought the fault lay with her.

Cam was silent a moment, then stood. "Again, I apologize. I just felt you should know why I did what I did."

Dodie looked up at him, not ready to have him go away. She stood as well. Without thinking about the wisdom of it, she placed her hand on his arm, needing, on one level, to recreate that connection.

"I wish I could tell you why Kelly did what she did," Dodie said. "I know, when she got the surgery, she said that she needed to talk to you. I'm wondering if she wants to make peace."

Cam released a humorless smile that had a patronizing twist. "Not gonna lie, I thought the same when I got her e-mail. But I think she has other things on her mind."

Dodie frowned her puzzlement. "So she hasn't apologized to you? If not, then what did she want?"

Cam sighed, shifting just enough to rest his hand on her waist, creating a slow spiral of appeal that she wanted nothing more than to give in to. Standing in front of her was the man, despite her marriage to Greg, that she thought of almost every day. A man who was resurrecting emotions she thought she would never feel again.

But too many questions hung between them yet. Too much uncertainty lay before them.

"She wants me to look at the farm's finances," he said. "She got a letter from the bank about some loans coming due."

Despite the distraction the warmth of his hand created, she latched on to what he said. "Loans? I thought the farm was free and clear. I remember Greg telling me how incredible it was to have so much equity with so little debt against it." Even as she spoke the words, she felt the slick of shame that she, Greg, and Kelly reaped the benefits that should have gone to Cam. At the very minimum, half. She'd always wondered why Cam had never asked for anything from the farm when it was his right to do so. At least, she had thought it was his right.

Greg never spoke about it. Never mentioned any obligation he felt toward Cam. And she thought nothing of it.

Until now.

"I thought so too, but I guess not. I'm not sure what Greg would have needed to borrow for. The tractor is the same one that Dad bought just before he died. So is the baler and the other equipment." He shrugged. "Maybe he bought more land?"

The conversation was shifting in a direction she didn't want to follow. She wanted to go back to what he had told her. Follow through on it and make sure she understood everything. "So when you broke up with me you already knew that Kelly had inherited the farm?"

He nodded, holding her gaze, and she caught a flash of pain in his eyes.

"I don't know how I would have responded, but I still wish you would have told me why," she said, her voice quiet. "It would have made things easier if I had known."

She slipped her hand up his arm, rested it on his shoulder, building on the attraction that sparked so easily between them.

"I wanted to, but part of me was ashamed. Hurt. I couldn't admit that my father thought so little of me that he handed my future over to Kelly. And the reality was my life went through a rough, hard haul to get to where I am. Lots of skipped meals and living hand-to-mouth. I didn't want that for you. There were times I missed you so bad I thought of calling you, but you were married to Greg."

She swallowed down her own shame. Her own guilt.

To tell him what had been weighing on her marriage, hanging over her and Greg's relationship. "You need to know that I had a reason for marrying Greg."

"Loneliness?"

She released a harsh laugh, hoping, praying that he would understand.

"Probably that's what caused the chain of events. I was sad. Depressed. Two months after you left, Greg came over with a couple of bottles of wine. To console me, he said. I thought he was being understanding. But..." She struggled with the next words. "I drank too much. Greg and I spent the night together. Two months later I discovered I was pregnant. So we got married right away. But then I had a miscarriage."

His sharp intake of breath cut through her shame. She couldn't look at him, the old disgrace and guilt rising up once again. She had struggled so hard to find forgiveness for herself and for Greg. It took her time and long conversations with her sister to work her way through it.

"Oh, Dodie, I'm so sorry. That must have been so difficult."

His unexpected sympathy caught her off guard. She blinked, trying to reconcile his words with her shame. All she could do was nod.

"And Greg must have been disappointed," he continued. "I know he wanted kids."

"I just told you I was intimate with your brother. Before we got married." Her shame kept her gaze averted. "Why are you being so kind?"

Cam cupped her chin in his hand, lifting her face, his eyes holding hers. "I'm not judging you for that," he said. "You were alone, and Greg should have known better."

"But it wasn't just him. I was a participant."

"I understand that."

"I don't think you do." She struggled to make sense of what he was saying, wondering how he could be so calm. So forgiving. It had haunted her for all of their marriage. Had been like a stain. A black cloud.

And had created the crack through which her old feelings for Cam would seep through.

"I felt so guilty about it," she said, trying to make him understand.

"Of course you would, but I know how persuasive Greg can be and how persistent. When you and I were dating, he often told me that I didn't deserve you. That he didn't care how it happened, some day he would get you back." He pressed his lips together, his thumb caressing her face. "And it looks like he did what he said he would."

Dodie could only stare at him, relief and remorse battling with each other. The burden she'd been carrying all this time. She wanted to protest again, still not believing that he was so quick to forgive her.

But he shifted his thumb to her mouth. Stopping her.

To her dismay, she felt the prickle of tears in her eyes. For her entire marriage to Greg, she felt tossed and torn. After she lost the baby, Greg had been caring, gentle, and understanding. And, she found out later, relieved.

She looked deep into Cam's caring eyes and the old emotions flooded through her. Free now.

She lifted herself up, drew his head down, and kissed his loving, generous mouth.

CAM HELD DODIE CLOSE, hardly daring to believe what had just happened.

He closed his eyes, burying his face in her hair, inhaling the various scents that were peculiarly Dodie. Pulled her close against him, her heart beating against his.

"Is this happening?" he asked, pressing a kiss on the warm, soft skin behind her ear. Letting his lips linger on her neck. "You and me?"

"I've never stopped thinking of you," Dodie said, her cheek now resting on his chest, her hand cradling his neck. "And that's what made my marriage to Greg a struggle."

Cam didn't want to talk anymore. He captured her lips with his again. He couldn't hold her close enough. Couldn't spend enough time with her to fill the emptiness that had haunted him all their time apart.

Finally, they drew away, catching their breath, letting their hearts slow.

Neither spoke for a long while. Just enjoyed this reunion. This wonderful connection.

Dodie rested her hands on his shoulders, her eyes holding his. "And now? Now what?"

"I've still got my tour."

Dodie nodded, acknowledging this. "And then?"

The words came out just above a whisper, and Cam knew what it had cost her to ask. The more time they spent together, the more time he spent back here in Millars Crossing, the more time at the old farm, the more he toyed with the idea of staying. He had money set aside to put a down payment on the farm. The tour would give him even more.

Could he buy it? Would he come back?

As he brushed another distracted kiss over Dodie's forehead, the question that had been edging around the back of his mind inched forward. Established itself.

"I'm not sure," was all he said. "My manager is still nagging at me to do that world tour after."

"How long would that take?"

"A year."

He caught the disappointment in her eyes and stroked away the frown on her forehead. "I'm not sure I want to go. I'm tired of running around. I know there's a young, very talented guy who is itching to take over from me."

This netted him a faint smile.

"And what would you do if you didn't tour?" Again that tentative tone in her voice. That slow movement to questions she didn't dare voice.

"I'd write songs," he said, letting himself linger on the thought. "I write most of the stuff we sing now. It would be a change of pace to just find a spot to do it that would feed my soul. To stay in one place. Get settled." He gave her a gentle smile, feeling as if the two of them were shifting back and forth, a delicate dance, not sure how much to give or show.

Did he dare?

She just told you she missed you. That she thought of you the entire time you were gone.

"I think the farm could be a great place to do it," she said.

He stroked her cheek, still smiling. "And I think you would be right." As soon as he spoke the words he felt an easing of the restlessness that had gripped him from the day he walked away from here.

"Would you be able to buy the farm?" she asked, her eyes still holding his as a gentle breeze lifted a strand of her hair, let it caress her face. He stroked it gently aside and tucked it behind her ear.

"Financially or emotionally?"

"Both, I guess."

He took her hand and held it between his, tracing a faint scar she had told him came from when she and Janie had fought over a pair of scissors. He knew so much about her.

"I have money set aside. Once I do this North American tour, I could have enough to get me started." He stood back to look at her.

She shifted away from him and walked back to the bench. Sat down again.

He wasn't sure what to say, but sensed she was waiting for something from him. Some commitment?

Did he dare make it?

He looked at her now, sitting quietly, her arms folded, feet crossed as she lounged on the bench, looking not at him, but at her garden as if drawing strength from it.

He watched her, let his eyes drift over her familiar, beautiful face. As he turned from looking at her to letting his eyes wander over her yard, the cozy little house and then, beyond that, to the jagged peaks of the Rocky Mountains he could just glimpse through a break in the trees, he felt as if his feet were growing roots. Settled.

He blew out a sigh, then turned back to Dodie.

"Do you want me to stay?" he asked.

"Do you want to stay?" she countered.

He realized her question meant that he had been the one to leave her. He had to be the one to make the declaration.

"Yes. I want to stay. I want to stay here."

He wasn't ready to take it further than that. But the implication lay heavily between them. If he stayed, they would have time to renew and grow their relationship.

And that was something he wanted very much.

"Let's go check the resin on those canoes," he said, returning to more practical matters.

Dodie pushed herself to her feet, giving him a gentle smile. "Sounds good. Maybe if you have time, we can work on the other canoe while we wait for the first one to dry."

"I have time," he said. "Right now, I've got all kinds of time."

And with another smile that held a promise to him, she walked back to the shop.

He was right behind her.

CHAPTER TEN

———— ⚜ ————

*D*odie pulled up to the farmhouse, shooting a quick glance in her rearview mirror. She was surprised when Cam said he would come along. She guessed he wanted to visit with Kelly.

He parked his truck right beside hers, flashing her a quick smile. Her heart went into overdrive and she tried not to flush. She returned his smile with one of her own, feeling a little self-conscious. Overly aware of him as he walked around his truck toward her.

"I'm glad you came along," she said, embarrassed at how breathless she sounded.

"Gives me a chance to spend a little more time with you as well as Kelly," he returned. He stroked her cheek with the back of his knuckles, a gentle, intimate gesture that spoke of an ease of being together. "Though you're more of a draw than Kelly is."

For a moment she thought he would kiss her, but then the

sound of a vehicle coming down the driveway drew both their attention.

And Dodie's heart sank.

It was her mother.

She clenched and unclenched her hands, unable to keep herself from glancing at Cam to catch his reaction. He looked over as well, just in time to see Tilly Westerveld park her car beside his truck and get out.

She was smiling at them, but Dodie could see it was forced. Not such a surprise. Her mother had never approved of Cam. When he left and Dodie got back together with Greg, Tilly was the second happiest mother in Millars Crossing. The first being Kelly.

"How wonderful to see you," Tilly said to Cam, walking over and holding out her hand, always exuding the politeness she had instilled in her children.

"Good to see you as well, Mrs. Westerveld," Cam said, shaking her hand.

"Thanks for bringing supper," Dodie said.

"Yes, I thought we could all eat together," her mother said. But as she did, she shot Cam a sideways glance, as if not too impressed with the fact that he was there as well.

"I need to get some work done," Dodie said with forced enthusiasm. She felt like Cam's kiss still burned on her lips. And the imprint of his fingers on her cheeks. Then she shook her hair back, reminding herself she wasn't a kid anymore. She didn't have to justify her actions to anybody.

"I know, but you also need to eat," her mother said.

"I can help you take the food inside," Cam said.

"That would be lovely," her mother said.

"I'll go see how Kelly is doing." Dodie didn't want to leave Cam and her mother alone, but Cam was a big boy and he could take care of himself.

It was just that everything was so tentative between them

right now. She wasn't sure where it was going, but she knew that the old feelings she thought she had suppressed had returned with a vengeance.

Kelly was sitting in the easy chair beside her bed reading when Dodie came inside.

"My mom is here with dinner," Dodie said. "I'm sure you're hungry, so why don't we get you to the table?"

Kelly's wide smile showed how thankful she was for the diversion. "That would be so wonderful. It's been a long, quiet day."

Again Dodie tried not to take that on. She had work to do and now, thanks to Cam's help, it looked like she would finish on time.

"Are you sure you can manage?" Dodie tried not to hover as she walked alongside her mother-in-law while she maneuvered her walker through the living room to the kitchen table.

"I'm fine," Kelly said, giving her a smile. "I'm doing better than I did yesterday."

"I'll just set the table," Dodie said. "My mom and Cam are just bringing supper in."

She hurried to the window to see what was happening. Thankfully, Cam and her mother were carrying the dishes up the walk. But she also sensed that something else had happened.

She once again sent up a prayer for peace and patience. She didn't know what else to pray for, her feelings were still in such a muddle.

And yet for the first time in years she felt a sense of hope. She wanted nothing interfering with that.

As she got the plates out of the cupboard, the back door opened and she heard Tilly and Cam's voices as they came inside. She paused, listening, but they sounded polite and upbeat. She even heard her mom chuckle.

A few minutes later a casserole and a salad were sitting in the middle of the table, an apple pie was cooling on the counter, and everyone was seated.

Kelly smiled as her gaze ticked from Dodie to Tilly and then Cam. "How wonderful to have a group of people around my table. That hasn't happened for a while."

"And I'm glad that Dan is out of town right now," Tilly said. "Gave me the best excuse ever to come over here and spend time with you."

Kelly turned to Cam. "Would you be willing to open in prayer?"

"Of course." Cam glanced over at Dodie and gave her a reassuring smile. Then he bowed his head and everyone else followed suit.

"Thank You, Lord, for wonderful food, friends, and family. Thank You for community and how we are supported by each other. Your love is everlasting and boundless and we see that in all the people You bring into our lives. Help us to be the kind of people You desire us to be. Bless this food and may it strengthen us. Be with Kelly and her recuperation. Help us to use what we have been given to help those who have less. Amen."

Dodie didn't realize she was holding her breath until he was finished. She knew Cam's prayer wasn't directed to her mother or his stepmother or even her. The sincerity in his voice moved her and, at the same time, gave her a feeling of rightness.

He was a good man.

As she opened her eyes, she caught her mother's surprised look. As if she couldn't believe he could offer up such a simple yet heartfelt prayer.

"Thank you for that," she said to Cam, giving him a gracious smile.

"I'm always thankful the Lord understands what I'm

trying to say. I'm also thankful for His love for the struggling sinner." Cam returned her smile, holding her gaze as if trying to tell her something.

Tilly looked thoughtful, then gave a gentle nod. "I think it's something we all need to be thankful for."

Dodie could hardly believe what she was hearing, but the tension in her neck relaxed. Her mother had never liked Cam and had never hidden her displeasure when Dodie was dating him. Now she was smiling at him.

"So when do you think you'll be able to rejoin our walking group?" Tilly asked Kelly as she served up the casserole. Dodie passed the salad around.

"I'm hoping in a few weeks," Kelly said. "And hopefully once we get the farm sold and I move into town, it'll be much easier for me to join you regularly."

"I'm very excited about that," Tilly said. "Maybe you can even take up quilting."

"One step at a time," Kelly said with a chuckle. "But I have to say how thankful I am for Dodie's help. I don't think I could've managed without her."

"I know I'm a bit prejudiced, but she is a treasure, and I'm sure an invaluable help." Tilly gave Dodie a smile. "So when will you be putting the farm up for sale?"

"Cam is looking into a few things for me before I list it," Kelly said, glancing at him. "I have the auctioneer lined up, but I don't think I'll get him to sell the farm."

Cam wiped his mouth and cleared his throat. "Speaking of listing the farm, have you spoken with the Sutton family? I understand they rent the land."

Kelly's eyes flicked from Dodie to Cam, then down. Her cheeks flushed as she shook her head.

Dodie wondered what was going on. She looked uncomfortable.

"From my point of view, because they are the renters,"

Cam continued, "I would think you should speak to them first."

"I... I will... I just..." Kelly pressed her lips together as if trying to gain her composure. "I will talk to them, before I talk to the real estate agent. I just need to get a few things cleared up first." She shot a quick glance to Cam, then down to her plate again. "Remember, we talked about this."

Dodie wondered what they had talked about. Cam seemed to know.

"And how is Mr. Westerveld doing?" Cam asked Tilly, switching the conversation to a more comfortable topic. "You said he was out of town."

"He's off playing golf with bigwigs from some construction company," Tilly said.

"And I don't know if you remember, but my mother isn't much for golfing," Dodie said.

"I seem to remember that," Cam said. "I have to agree with you, Tilly. Golf isn't on my list of favorite things to do."

"So you don't play golf when you're out touring?"

"No. Mostly I find a quiet place to sit so I can write. Work on my songs."

Tilly gave him a considering look. "Really. And no night-clubbing?"

Cam rolled his eyes. "I can't imagine a worse way to spend my time."

He, Kelly, and Dodie's mom chatted, the three of them chuckling at times. Dodie was more than content to watch and make sure everyone's glasses stayed full. She cleared the table when they were all done.

Brought out dessert.

And enjoyed the surprising ambience. While her mother wasn't exactly treating Cam like an old friend, she was being kind. Asking a lot of questions about life on the road as a touring band. Asking him about his upcoming trip.

Cam seemed ready to oblige. As Dodie cut up the pie, he spoke of how busy his life was. What was all involved and the logistics. Part of her wished no one else was around so she could ask those same questions herself. Cuddle up to him on a couch in her house and just have ordinary conversation. Make connections.

Yet seeing her mother, who had at one time disliked Cam so much, engage with him eased away a tension that had gripped her when she and Cam were dating the first time.

After dessert, Cam got up and cleared the table, motioning for Dodie to sit. "I'll take care of the dishes," he said. "You visit with Kelly and your mother."

She wanted to protest, but it would look rude.

"And how is your garden coming?" her mother asked while Cam worked behind her. "Have you moved your plants from your greenhouse yet?"

"Yes. They're thriving. The flowerpots are doing well. I'll be putting them out next week. I don't think it will freeze anymore."

"I always find it so amazing what you've done with that property," Kelly put in.

"She's got quite the green thumb," her mother said. "And it helps to be such a homebody. Makes it easier to stay on top of weeds." Tilly turned to Cam. "Have you seen what Dodie has done to her and Greg's place? It's like a little paradise."

"I have. It's beautiful."

Dodie could hear Cam working behind her, but she kept her gaze on her mother, sensing something else was going on.

"I know Greg often asked her to come along on his trips when seeding was done, but she always wanted to stay behind," Tilly continued. "She doesn't enjoy leaving."

"Mother, you make me sound like some hermit," Dodie protested.

"Not a hermit," Tilly said, patting her hand. "Just a home-body. And that's a good thing. Being happy and content in your own space is a gift. You're just like me that way. I love working in my garden and never like going along with your father on his trips."

"Greg's trips were always to Vegas," Dodie said, shuddering at the memory. Greg always came back full of stories of the shows he saw and the people he met. He would show her pictures of the Strip, the massive and overdone hotels. The lights and the busyness all hours of the night.

Nope. Not for her.

"I can't imagine Greg in Vegas," Cam said as he loaded up the dishwasher.

"He started going when that equipment salesman wanted to do more business with him and lured him with a free trip," Kelly said. "Then he and his friend, Paul, the accounts manager at the bank, started going. He always enjoyed it, and it was a good way for him to blow off some steam."

"Have you ever been to Vegas?" Tilly asked Cam.

He came back to the table and picked up the napkins. "My band and I opened for a group in Vegas, but it was off the strip. Wasn't my cup of tea either."

"You and Greg were different in so many ways," Kelly said.

On the surface it sounded like an offhand comment, but beneath it Dodie heard an echo of everything she'd noticed in Kelly since Cam came back. An echo of the things Cam had touched on.

Greg was her special, beloved child. Cam, not so much.

"They each have their gifts," Dodie said.

"Speaking of gifts and talents, Cam, has Dodie shown you the guitar she made?"

Tilly's question surprised Dodie, and once again she wasn't sure what her mother was doing.

"Yes, I saw it," Cam said, bringing the napkins to the kitchen counter. "It's amazing. Has a beautiful sound."

"You think so?"

Dodie shot her mother a questioning glance, but her mother ignored her.

"I do."

"I think she should make more of them. She might make more money selling them than selling canoes," Tilly said.

"I know I'd be interested in one." Cam sat down across from Dodie, flashing her a warm smile.

"Really. And you would take it on tour with you?"

"Okay, Mom. That's enough. I don't need you to be my business manager," Dodie said, a warning tone in her voice, guessing where this was going.

"Can't a mother be proud of her daughter?"

"A mother can," Dodie said. "But a mother can't start peddling work for her daughter."

Tilly's frown showed Dodie that her mother got the hint. She wrinkled her nose and crossed her arms. Both signs that she would listen, but she wasn't happy about it.

"I will. When it's finished," Cam said, still holding Dodie's eyes, apparently unfazed by her mother's blatant huckstering.

"Well then, I'll have to finish it," she said, her voice quiet.

They were both silent a moment as their eyes met.

And for a few heartbeats, Dodie felt as if they were the only ones in the room. Everything else fell away, even her mother and mother-in-law.

Then Tilly, as if noticing the moment, cleared her throat and got to her feet, her chair screeching on the ceramic tile of the floor.

"Why don't we go sit in the living room," Tilly said to Kelly. "We need to catch up."

"That would be lovely." Kelly glanced over at Dodie. "Why don't you come and join us?"

Dodie felt trapped as her mother's expectant look matched Kelly's.

Then she made a decision.

"Thanks, but I have to get back to the shop. There's a few things I need to take care of." She looked over at Cam. "Do you mind coming and help me out? I need to take that one canoe off the mold."

Which wasn't entirely true, but her mother didn't need to know that.

"Sure, I don't mind," Cam said. "I should get going anyhow. I need to call my manager."

"About your tour?" Tilly asked.

"That and a few other things." Cam gave her a polite smile and Tilly gave him a tight nod.

Dodie brushed a quick kiss over her mother's cheek then Kelly's then hurried out of the house before either one could say anything more.

As she walked down the steps, she heard Cam's footsteps right behind her on the veranda. When she got to her truck, she stopped and faced him.

He came close, smiling down at her as she backed up against the driver's door.

"So, maybe you can translate for me. Does your mother like me or hate me as much as she did before? I couldn't figure out which it was." He placed his hands on the truck, hemming her in.

Just the way she liked it.

She could feel the warmth emanating off him. Caught the scent of his hair. Woodsy, masculine.

Cam.

"I wish I knew," Dodie admitted, resting her hands on his

waist. "She seemed interested in talking to you about your music."

"Or that could just be a way to remind you of my wicked, wandering ways."

"I don't think she sees you as wicked."

"Maybe not now, but I think she used too."

Dodie couldn't refute that. While she and Cam dated, she heard too many comments about how irresponsible Cam was. How he was so much work for Kelly. Even when he got older and no longer went to school, Tilly had intimated that Cam wasn't a good prospect.

And as those thoughts coalesced, an icy finger of reality trickled down her spine.

"I wonder if Kelly told my mom about your dad's will."

Cam frowned. "Why would she do that?"

"They're best buds. Kelly might have mentioned something to her. So my mom might have known that you were getting cut out."

Cam's expression grew suddenly hard, and Dodie regretted bringing it up. "Maybe. Maybe she knew I would end up with nothing and Greg, potentially with everything."

"She often told me that Greg would be better able to provide for me, which always puzzled me. And after your father died, she pushed for Greg harder."

"But now I'm making money." He forced a grin, but Dodie could see that it was work for him. "Maybe now I'm a better prospect."

Dodie felt a quiver of resentment with her mother and sympathy for Cam.

"I always thought you were a better prospect from the beginning," she said, pulling his head down for a quick kiss.

She stifled her own guilt at what she'd told him yesterday. Her confession.

"I'm glad about that," Cam said. "And what about now?"

"Even more," she returned. But even as she spoke the words, a question niggled below her confident declaration.

Would he stay? Did she dare carry on with this growing and changing relationship if she didn't know that?

Then he kissed her again, and the questions blew away, like dust in a summer storm.

DODIE GAVE the porch swing on her deck a push with her foot, then took another sip of water. The sun was hovering above the trees. Evening was coming.

And Cam sat across from her, his booted feet stretched out in front of him, his hands clasped behind his head. She smiled at the sight. Greg so seldom sat out here with her that images of him didn't intrude into the moment.

She didn't know if it was her hopeful heart projecting her emotions onto him, but he looked content. Happy. She wanted to comment on it but she thought it would break the mood.

Yesterday, after their kiss, they had returned to the shop. Once there, he had been all business. They'd planed the rest of the cedar strips and glued them together over the form. Then sanded and sanded and sanded some more. As they worked Dodie felt the pressure on her ease off. Cam had promised to help her until they finished the last canoe.

She hadn't dared ask him when he was leaving for his tour. For now, the fact that he had cancelled his trip to Mexico to help her out had given her the glimmer of hope. Allowed her to think about a future.

"I forgot how quiet it is out here," Cam said. "Dad and I used to come here once in a while."

"Did you ever go fishing?"

"If we did, it was off the dock. Dad was scared of water.

Could never figure out why I would want to build a canoe that would take me out onto it." A smile slipped across his well-shaped lips. Then his eyes turned to hers and she couldn't look away. And the hope his kiss had created grew.

"I know. I love it so much here." Dodie gave the swing another push. "If you listen, you should be able to hear a loon."

Cam's smiled deepened, enhancing the faint crinkles at the corners of his eyes. "A loon?" He shook his head as he eased out a wistful sigh. "I haven't heard that in years. Will we hear it better if we get closer to the lake?"

"We can."

"Then let's go for a walk." He got up and held his hand out.

She took it, a gentle calm washing over her as she let his warm hand engulf hers. Letting his very presence give her a moment to dream.

The two of them, living here, together.

"We can watch the sun go down and look for the birds," he continued.

"I know there's a couple pairs hanging out at the edge of the lake," she said, hoping she didn't sound as breathless as she felt. "I found their nest this spring when I was canoeing."

He released her hand as he followed her down the narrow path to the lake, the dusk creating intimate shadows.

Dodie tried not to let her feelings jump too far ahead. For now, this was just a simple walk with an old friend, she told herself.

Cam never will be simply an old friend.

Especially not when his merest touch stirred feelings she hoped had become dormant.

The forest opened and in a few more steps they were at the lake. The sun sent a glow of orange light across the mirror-smooth surface of the water. Her canoe was tied up to the wooden pier jutting out into the lake.

"Is that the canoe we made?" Cam asked. "The one your dad uses?"

She replied with a quick nod, her hands shoved in her back pockets as she rocked back and forth.

"You want to take it out? I'd like to see if it still works."

Dodie chuckled. "Canoes don't work or not work," she said with a teasing tone. "They're a vessel that depends on the skill of the paddler."

"Well, I'm no skillful paddler," Cam said. "But I'd like to try again. It's been years since I sat in a canoe."

"That doesn't give me much confidence," Dodie said, trying to keep the conversation light. Trying to keep the distance between herself and Cam.

"Oh, I have excellent balance," Cam said. "I can hold a guitar, sing, and walk at the same time."

"Critical skills for canoeing."

She was thankful for the quick return to their easy give-and-take. It eased the faint tension that hummed between them whenever they were together.

"The paddles are in the canoe," Dodie said. "The life-jackets are back at the house."

"I won't drown in this lake," Cam said. "I think we can do without lifejackets."

Dodie had to agree. She seldom paddled with a lifejacket, much to the chagrin of her mother and sister. They were worrywarts. She knew how to swim, and the lake wasn't the bitter cold ocean. She wouldn't get hypothermia. Not in the summer anyway. She loved paddling without the bulk of her life jacket.

She strode down the dock, her footsteps echoing on the wood, the vibration sending faint ripples from the posts into the glass-like stillness of the lake.

"You're the novice, so you have to go up front." Dodie untied the rope and held the canoe steady.

"You just want to be in control."

"Of course. What's wrong with that?" Dodie returned.

He flashed her a smile and gingerly climbed into the canoe. It wobbled a bit, and he clung to the gunwales. She tried not to chuckle.

"Not as easy as it looks, is it, landlubber?" she teased.

He shot her a wry look as he leaned back to pick up a paddle. "I am well up to the task."

"We'll see about that," she said. "Just remember, I call the shots. So when I call change, you change, or you'll end up in the water."

"Aye, aye, Captain." He gave her a mock salute, then laid the paddle across the gunwales while she got in.

Dodie caught her balance, then sat down and used her paddle to push them away from the dock.

As she steered the canoe away from the shore, she felt a familiar peace steal over her.

"Where are we headed?" he asked as he dipped the paddle into the water, pulling a long hard stroke.

"This isn't a race," Dodie said. "You don't need to work so hard. Besides, that makes it tricky for me to steer, and I feel like I have to keep up."

"I thought you were the expert," Cam returned. He shot a look over his shoulder and she grinned at his expression.

"Well then, I'll just have to up my game," she said.

Cam turned back, laughing. They paddled in silence for a while as the earth wheeled, the sun dipping below the tree line.

Tension eased from her neck and shoulders as the only sound was the gentle dip and drip of paddles in and out of the water. Being out on the lake always brought her peace. Though she loved Greg and over all they'd had a good relationship, the last few months of their marriage had been fraught with anxiety and stress. He was always uptight and snapped easily at her.

When she had tried to talk about it, he cut her off. He would tell her everything was fine and not to worry.

But there were many times when she heard him on the phone, angry, his voice tense. If she tried to find out what was happening, he would wave her out of the office.

She had learned to leave, to not engage him. On those days she would come to the lake, slip into her canoe, and start paddling. Finding the peace that fled their house with every unexpected phone call, every trip to town. She had to trust that he was right, as he had promised her.

Whenever she tried to talk to her mother about Greg, she got platitudes and reminders that marriage was difficult. That there were tough times in any relationship. Then her mother would list a litany of things she had to endure with Dodie's father.

"Where are those loons you were promising to show me?" Cam asked, breaking into her restless thoughts.

She gave a gentle shake of her head. "It's not like we're going to see some statue or some piece of art that waits for us. We don't go looking for the loons. We just wait till they show up."

"Well, I have to say I'm disappointed. I thought you had an in with these birds. That you could make them come on command."

Dodie laughed. It had always been so easy to be around Cam. He could laugh at himself. Sure, she caught glimpses of his famous temper from time to time, but never directed at her.

"Well then, I guess I'll just have to be patient." Cam glanced back at her "Can we change sides now?"

"Don't tell me you're tired already?" Dodie chided him.

"Just trying to maintain a balance," Cam said. "Something I've been told to do most of my life."

"Good advice." Dodie switched as well, steering the canoe toward a grouping of cattail bulrushes where she had found a nest earlier this spring. Maybe the loon and her babies were hiding in there.

And then she heard it.

The deep-throated, mournful call followed by a melancholy quiver echoing over the silence of the lake. A sound that called to her each time she heard it.

Cam stopped, laying his paddle across the gunwale, leaning forward as if to hear better.

Dodie did the same, and for a few moments they floated along, listening to the loons call back and forth.

Then as the last echoes faded away, Dodie saw another loon and two chicks low in the water dive beneath the surface.

"Where do you think they'll come up again?" Cam asked. His voice was quiet, as if he too understood the near holiness of this moment.

"It's anybody's guess." Dodie kept her paddle out of the water, waiting.

Then to her surprise they surfaced about ten meters from the canoe. Cam jerked, the canoe shifting with his sudden movement. But he steadied himself quick enough. He watched the loons as they slid silently through the water. Black heads with glowing eyes, black-and-white speckled wings, a symmetrical pattern peculiar to them. They floated low in the water, the mother's head slipping from side to side, watching her chicks, measuring the distance between them and the canoe. The curious chicks moved closer and closer and then suddenly the mother rose up again, her wings splashing in the water. She called out one more time. Then she ducked under the water, her chicks following her.

They both sat there silently, appreciating the miraculously beautiful thing they had just seen.

Cam slowly shook his head as if in wonder. "I've heard loons before but I didn't realize how much I miss that sound. It's haunting."

Dodie watched and saw the loons come up much farther away this time.

Cam's words echoed in her mind, expressing the emotion she always felt when she heard the birds.

"You might have to write a song about this," Dodie teased, dipping her paddle back in the water, propelling them a little farther along.

Cam glanced back to see which side she was paddling on, then followed suit.

"It would take me a long time to ponder on this, think about how to capture the moment, the feelings, and more importantly that sound."

"My dad taught me how to call loons," Dodie said.

She remembered sitting with her father on the pier as he showed her how to cup her hands just so and blow into them. It wasn't the same, but it was close enough that often the loons would call back.

Happy memories, reminding her of how much she loved being here. Being a part of the land, entrenching herself deep into the rhythms of nature.

They paddled on as Dodie tucked this moment away in her memory box.

To take out when Cam is gone?

"Show me some time," he said, scattering her thoughts. "But right now, I wouldn't mind going back. My arms are a little tired."

"Oh, come on, I thought stars like you were constantly lifting weights and bench pressing," Dodie teased.

"Only when I can get to the gym," Cam said as Dodie turned the canoe around, back to the pier.

"You're gonna have to install a gym in your new tour bus." She tried to speak the words casually. The simple recognition of the life he was returning to.

But even as she said it, she felt a surge of discontent in her soul. A lingering frustration. She knew she had no right to ask anything, but after spending the last week and a half together, she had seen a change come over him. He seemed to exude a gentle peace that he hadn't had when he first came.

They paddled in silence the rest of the way back, Dodie keeping up a steady but easy rhythm. She could have gone on for another hour or two, but watching Cam's back, watching his muscles move under his shirt as he handled the paddle, was more difficult than she wanted to admit.

So close, and yet so far.

It was dusk by the time they got to the pier. The trees were dark silhouettes against a glowing sky. Dodie steered them up alongside and held the canoe up against the dock.

"Grab the front rope and climb out carefully," she said. If you don't mind tying up, then I can get out."

Cam gingerly disembarked then crouched down and held the nose of the canoe as Dodie worked her way to the front. She laid her paddle on the dock and was about to clamber out when Cam reached out his hand.

She could've got out on her own, but she took his hand and let him help her out of the canoe.

But he didn't release her hand, and for a moment they stood there, inches away from each other. His eyes glinted in the semi-dark. Her heart expanded, and she couldn't find her breath. Cam laid his other hand on her neck, his fingers caressing the skin just above the collar of her shirt.

The silence beat between them, expectant, waiting.

Then Cam moved closer as she lifted her face. Their breaths mingled and their lips touched. Hesitant at first, as if trying to discover who they were now. What they were allowed to expect this time.

Cam groaned as he slid his hand from her neck down to her waist and pulled her closer. He released her hand, both his arms wrapped around her now, and she returned his embrace. Their lips were cool yet slowly warmed as they moved over each other, seeking, discovering.

So familiar. So comfortable.

His mouth slipped over her cheeks, gently raining kisses down to her neck, nuzzling her as he murmured her name. Dodie's head dropped back, weak, overwhelmed with emotion. Then Cam shifted his hands as they caught her face, his thumb stroking over her cheeks then her lips.

"I missed you so much," he whispered. Dodie looked deep into his eyes, saw the glint of passion burning there.

She didn't want to talk right now, didn't want words to come between them as they once had.

So she caught him by the neck and pulled his head down to hers again.

Long moments later, she pulled back.

Cam rested his forehead against hers, his breath coming quickly, displaying his own runaway emotions.

For a moment neither spoke, allowing what they just experienced to settle. To find its own way.

Dodie silenced all the questions swirling in her mind.

This was here, this was now.

And it felt so right.

It felt like coming home.

CHAPTER ELEVEN

*C*am stood in the back of the church, looking around. The Westervelds weren't here yet and neither was Dodie.

"There are some empty spots to your left." The usher joined him, handing him a bulletin. "I can show you."

"Thanks. I'm fine." Cam wasn't ready to acknowledge to some complete stranger, who probably knew Dodie well, that he was looking for her.

Besides, he wondered despite Tilly's seeming acceptance of him the other day how she would feel about him sitting with her darling daughter. The widow of her best friend's son.

He saw an empty seat and was about to enter the sanctuary when he heard his name called.

By Dodie.

He turned to see her coming toward him across the wide-open lobby, Kelly beside her using a walker.

"Kelly wanted to come to church today," Dodie said as they joined him.

Cam gave Dodie a gentle smile, then turned to Kelly. "I'm sure you missed being here."

"I did, so I asked Dodie if she would pick me up."

"You could have called me," he said, feeling a surge of protectiveness toward Dodie. He knew how much time she already devoted to his stepmother.

"I suppose," Kelly said, looking surprised, as if she had never thought about that.

"Well, we're all here," Dodie said. "Let's go in."

She seemed to assume that he would sit with them, and he wasn't about to protest. So he followed behind them to the nearest empty spot. Dodie helped Kelly sit down, then motioned for Cam to sit as well. He made a space between him and Kelly for Dodie.

As she settled in, she flashed him a smile. An ordinary smile. The kind that couples share.

He looked into her eyes and felt as if his life was shifting. As if he dared to make other plans.

They turned their attention back to the group who was gathering at the front. Same group as last time, Cam noticed.

One singer moved to the mike as he tuned his guitar, looking over the congregation. "I didn't notice last time, but I found out later that Cam Morgan is with us this Sunday. I hope he'll forgive our feeble attempts."

Cam shifted, feeling uncomfortable at the call-out. People knew who he was. He'd gotten stopped a few times when he was in town, but it always made him feel awkward. The attention was a new thing coming from more airplay of his band's songs on the radio ahead of their tour.

As far as he was concerned, he was just doing his thing.

"And after putting him on the spot, I would like to push things even further. An old friend of his, Finn Sutton, encouraged me to ask if he would join us. Finn said that Cam wouldn't mind at all."

Cam looked ahead to where the Sutton family usually sat in church. Sure enough, Finn was looking back, giving him a thumbs-up while Etta nudged him as if telling him to behave.

But now, Cam was on the spot. To say no would make him look like he thought himself too good for the people of Millars Crossing. To go up would be to draw attention to himself as a performer when the music was really supposed to bring the people of the church together to worship God.

"Just go up there," Dodie whispered, leaning close, squeezing his arm in a gesture of support. "I'd love to hear you sing."

Cam hesitated a moment then, when the couple ahead of him turned around and whispered their encouragement as well, he gave in. He moved carefully past Kelly who, no surprise, was frowning as if puzzled at the attention Cam was getting. He tried not to let it get to him. Kelly's reaction shouldn't matter to him. But as he strode up the carpeted aisle to the front, he couldn't help a slight moment of satisfaction. A chance to show her he had made a name for himself. That he was worthy.

"I hope you don't mind using my guitar," the lead singer mumbled, standing back from the mike as he handed it to him.

"What's your name?" Cam whispered.

"Shane. Shane DeRuiter," he said, flushing at the attention. "And I'm honored you're willing to come and play with us."

Not like he had much choice, but if Shane was honored, then Cam had to go with it.

"Our set list is on the iPad by the mike," Shane told him. "But you can play any of your songs you want. Our group knows them all."

Cam had received many accolades, as Sons of the Home-steaders became better known. But this, knowing that a small singing group in his old hometown knew and played his songs, made his heart beat with a sense of fulfillment even the largest audience had never given him.

"Some might not be appropriate," he said as he tuned the guitar and looked at the list. He knew the first two, but not the rest. "So let's go with the first ones you've got and then we can do one that the congregation probably knows by heart, like a couple of verses of 'How Great Thou Art.'" It was an old song but given the time he and Dodie spent outside yesterday, reconnecting with nature, he felt the song was appropriate.

"Okay. Sounds good." Shane stood back to let Cam go to the mike.

Cam sent up a quick prayer for strength and, he had to admit, patience with his "old friend" Finn who had put him in this spot. But as he stepped up to the mike and looked around the congregation, he felt a rush of joy and connection. This was his old community. People who knew him from when he was young. People who knew his parents, both his mother and his father. Teachers, leaders of youth group, people who had links to him in so many ways. Some tenuous, some stronger. Some positive, some not so positive.

Nevertheless, this was his community.

And as he strummed the first chords of the first song and he saw people smiling up at him, he felt a sense of belonging. Of coming home.

DODIE'S HEART soared as she listened to Cam singing. She wanted to sing along, but also wanted to just listen to him.

He used to sing when they were dating, belting out the country songs he loved listening to.

But now his voice had gotten deeper, richer, fuller. He had more confidence.

And as he sang, she felt some deep promise of joy and contentment wash over her.

But reality hovered. He was a singer with a band that was growing popular. A band that would leave for six months and then probably around the world for a year.

Always on the move.

For a few brief and wonderful moments, she had thought he might settle here. He had hinted at it the last time they talked.

But as she listened to him sing, as he effortlessly drew the music from the guitar he held, she knew talent like his shouldn't be left to languish in Millars Crossing.

The thought created a quiver in her soul and the prick of tears in her eyes.

The band sang the last verse of "How Great Thou Art" a cappella, and as the last notes of his rich baritone voice rang out through the auditorium, a few tears slipped from her eyes.

Cam relinquished the guitar to the other singer then walked back, head bowed, as if still thinking of the song he just sang. Then, to her surprise, the congregation of Millars Crossing did what had never been done before. They all stood and applauded.

And she joined them.

Cam gave a brief wave of his hand as if wishing they would stop, looking embarrassed. A reaction that surprised Dodie. He had been applauded before. She saw one of his concerts put up on YouTube. Whistling and clapping and cheering by the audience, and yet this small token of appreciation seemed to make him uncomfortable.

Then, as he joined her, and they sat down with the rest of the congregation, she couldn't stop herself. As they settled in the pew, she slipped her arm through his, moving to be close to him.

"That was amazing and so incredibly moving," she whispered in his ear.

His smile warmed her soul. As he squeezed her arm closer to his side, she felt a sense that the tension between them was growing, tightening. Since they had reconnected, she had tried not to look too far ahead. Tried to block it out.

She couldn't anymore.

They had to talk about the future.

The service flowed on and though Dodie took much of what Pastor Simons said to heart, she was far too aware of Cam beside her. And when people came to talk to him, she didn't leave, as if claiming him. At least for now.

Finn sauntered past, and she saw him give Cam a thumbs-up. Cam's only response was an eye roll and a shake of his head.

Finally she, Kelly, and Cam could leave. Tilly and her Aunt Dot joined them, chatting with Kelly.

"Do you want to come for lunch?" Tilly asked, glancing from Kelly to Dodie and Cam.

"We'd love to," Kelly responded with a smile.

Dodie could imagine her mother-in-law was more than ready to be out of the house and meeting other people. She didn't tire as easily.

But Dodie wasn't coming along.

"Cam and I have other plans," she said, looking her mother in the eye as if challenging her to say anything about that.

She didn't look in Cam's direction to catch his reaction. Didn't matter. She needed to talk to him. In private.

"I see," was all Tilly said.

"And I was wondering if either you or Aunt Dot would be willing to bring Kelly home afterwards?" May as well get all the time out of them she could.

"Of course, my dear," Aunt Dot said with a broad smile. "That way we can visit and gossip as much as we want."

And Dodie was sure her little pronouncement would be dissected and discussed as well.

No matter.

She followed behind her mother, aunt, and mother-in-law, supervising as they helped Kelly into Tilly's car. Cam folded up her walker and put it into the back of Tilly's vehicle.

Then she waited, watching as her mother and aunt drove off the parking lot.

Only then did she turn to Cam.

He was looking at her, one eyebrow lifted quizzically. "We have plans? That sounds ominous."

She heard the uncertainty in his voice and wasn't sure how to assure him.

"We need to talk. But I'm not doing that here. I can see more people want to speak with you. Why don't we meet at my place? I can make lunch."

"And maybe go for another canoe ride?" he asked.

"Maybe," was all she could manage.

Now that she had made the commitment, she couldn't stop a trembling deep in her soul. Was she doing the right thing? Would this all blow up in her face?

But as she drove to her house, she knew she had to get this off her chest. She and Cam were getting too close. They weren't teenagers anymore, playing around, trying to see if this relationship would work. They both had expectations and obligations, and she needed to know what to expect.

Eighteen nervous minutes later she heard Cam's truck

pull up on the yard and she came out to meet him. She had a pot of soup she had canned warming in the slow cooker, and some bread she had baked this morning sitting under a tea towel. It could wait.

She wiped her damp hands over her skirt as Cam got out of the truck, his eyes holding hers. He walked toward her, his hands in his pockets, his posture nonchalant, but she saw the lines of tension bracketing his mouth.

"Let's walk to the lake," she said, giving him what she hoped was a reassuring smile.

Maybe he thought she was getting payback. Now she would tell him she couldn't give him what he needed.

And, in a way, she couldn't. She couldn't imagine herself living his life. She shot a quick glance around the property, feeling, as she always did, a sense of completion. Of rooted belonging. Thinking of leaving this gave her a physical ache.

They were quiet as they walked, single file, down the path. Each step closer to the dock where Dodie wanted to have this conversation felt weighted with a mixture of dread and hope.

They got to the end and Dodie sat down, cross-legged, draping her skirt around her legs. Cam sat down beside her, letting his legs dangle off the boards, his feet just skimming the water.

"Be careful you don't get those fancy boots wet," she teased, her voice breathless.

"I've got another pair."

"Ostrich skin?"

"Eww. Nope. Good old sturdy tooled cowhide."

She smiled at that, pressed her lips together.

Please, Lord, she prayed, give me the right words. Help me find the way through this.

"I loved listening to you this morning," she said.

"I enjoyed playing. It was quite a rush to look over the audience and know most everyone there. And to be singing songs I wrote in front of old school friends who used to tease me about my playing satisfied the tiny corner of my mind that always hoped I could show them." He gave her a cautious smile. "I know it's petty, but there it is. However, even more, it was wonderful to sing in front of you. To sing for the Lord. Both were a highlight that I'll never forget."

His words held an echo of leaving.

She took a quick breath then plunged into what she wanted to say. "When do you have to leave for your tour?"

Cam folded his hands together, leaning forward. "The tour starts in a month, but I want to get to Vancouver two weeks before that to rehearse. Put together our set lists. Go over equipment one last time. Make sure we've got everything in place."

"Isn't the tour already set up?"

"Oh, yeah. Has been for months."

"And what will happen after this tour?"

Now Cam was quiet. "My manager has been nagging at me about setting up a world tour."

"And how long would that take?"

"It would be for at least a year."

"So, six months for this one and then another year?" The thought sent panic spiraling down her gut. Could she be apart from him that long?

"That was the plan." Then Cam shifted, turning to her. "Until I came here."

His words stilled her breath and that tiny glimmer of hope grew.

"What are you saying?"

Cam straightened, taking one of Dodie's hands in his, once again caressing it. "I had my plans laid out. I was more than willing to take the second tour. It would be fantastic exposure and would send our band international. Would be significant money. But now, I don't want to go."

Dodie's heart scrambled in her chest, her breath stuck in her throat.

"You don't?" The question came out like a squeak.

"No. I can't get out of the one ahead, but the world tour one is still in limbo. My manager has been after me for the past few days to decide. But I think I'll say no."

"What will you do?"

"What do you want me to do?" he parried.

She felt like they were performing some delicate dance. He moved forward, now it was her turn. A few tentative steps and then back.

Another prayer, another calming breath.

Just say it.

The vulnerable part of her held back. The memory of him walking away could still sear her soul. But now that she knew why he had done it-

"I want you to come back after that tour and stay here." The words tumbled out in a blended rush of hope and fear.

His smile crawled across his soft lips. "That's what I want to do too."

She swallowed, relief making her weak. "I'm glad."

"Are you?"

"Yes. Yes, I am. I'm thrilled. Happy. So happy."

"I would be gone for six months," he told her. "But I'm calling my manager tonight and telling him to cancel the world tour. And as soon I can, I'll be back. And then we'll get married."

"Here?"

"Where else would I go? You're here and you're all I want."

He disentangled his hand from hers and curved it around her neck. They both moved at the same time, hungry lips meeting halfway, arms entangling around each other.

Sealing the deal.

After some time Dodie pulled back, her hand cupping his beloved face. "Six months isn't that long."

"No. It isn't."

"And while you're gone, I can plan our wedding."

Cam looked sorrowful at that.

"I mean, unless-" Had she heard him wrong? "Are you okay?"

"I am. But I shouldn't have blurted that out. I should have done a proper proposal. I even had one planned from the last time."

Dodie smiled at his discomfort. "I don't need a fancy proposal. I don't even want a fancy wedding."

Her thoughts ticked back to her wedding to Greg that had been, in her mind, over the top. But it had been what her mother and Kelly wanted. So she went along with their plans, when secretly she would've just as soon gotten married here. On this yard.

Then Cam took her hand. "I don't have a ring, but I'm still doing this properly. Dorothea Westerveld slash Morgan. I want to be by your side the rest of your life. I want to wake up to you each morning and kiss you good night each evening, and maybe in between. Will you marry me?"

Dodie looked down at him, blinking back tears of joy. Then she hugged him tight, burying her face in his neck. "Yes. Of course I will."

They kissed again, then Dodie leaned back, clinging to Cam's hands as if afraid he would leave.

"It will be a struggle to be apart from you," Dodie said.

"It's going to be brutal, but it will end. It's only six months." Cam shifted so he was sitting beside her, his arm around her once again.

Only. That made it sound less than what it actually would be. By the time Cam came back it would be winter. The thought depressed her. But still, he would be back.

"I'll have to talk to Kelly," he continued. "I have enough saved up that I could put some down on the farm. What I make off this tour would buy me livestock and some more equipment and put the crop in. I want to see if Kelly would be willing to carry me for the first two years. Once I get a calf crop and a grain crop, I can finance and pay her back."

"You sound like you had this all planned."

"I've been playing around with it."

She could hardly believe they were having this conversation, sitting here on the pier. Hardly believe he had already thought of their future as well. But then something else occurred to her to dampen her ebullient spirits.

"Do you think Kelly will go along with it?"

He was quiet a moment, then slowly nodded. "I think so. Right now she's worried about some letter the bank sent her about the farm's finances, so I'll have to look into that."

"You don't seem too concerned."

"I'm not. Dad had the farm paid off. The only loans he carried were against the equipment, which we still have."

"But Kelly hired that Devon Collier guy to do the auction. What will you do about him?"

Cam brushed his thumb over her cheek. "I'm kind of excited to tell him we don't need him anymore."

"Now, Cam, where is your Christian charity?"

"I will tell him with love as my motive." Cam smiled.

"I'm sure you can pull it off."

"I'm a very loving person." Then his face grew serious as he took her hands in his. "And I'm in love with you. I don't think I ever stopped."

His words dove into her heart, creating a surge of love

and tangled relief. "I love you too," she said before he kissed her again.

And again.

And once more, as in the distance, the loon called out its melancholy song.

CHAPTER TWELVE

"*A*re you sure you can manage the takeover of the farm?" Kelly frowned as she asked Cam the question.

She was sitting in her chair downstairs. Home care had just left, and she was drinking her tea when Cam came into the house. The sun shining through the windows was like a promise, and Cam's heart was full.

Last night after he left Dodie's, he felt as if he were floating.

Now, sitting with Kelly and making plans brought him back to earth, but in oh such a good way.

"I believe I can if you're willing to not take a full payment right away."

Kelly nodded, as if considering this. "So how would I buy my house?"

"If we buy you a new place, we'd only need a five percent

189

down payment. I could manage that with the cash I have on hand."

"And what about the farm debts?"

"Dad had this place paid off before he died, and I'm sure Greg borrowed some to buy that fancy new tractor sitting outside. I would bring that into the dealer and trade it on the smaller unit." The last two nights he had been sitting and crunching numbers but was just going on guesswork.

"I have an appointment this morning with your accounts manager to talk about the financial situation," he continued. "I'll know more what I'm dealing with after that."

"I'm glad you're able to do that. I was always thankful that Greg took that all over."

She was quiet a moment, and Cam wondered if she was thinking about her son. His brother.

The glistening of tears in her eyes showed him he was right. "I really miss him sometimes," she said, her voice trembling. Then she drew in a slow breath. "And I know I spoiled him. Yesterday Tilly, Dot, and I were talking, and they told me that I was wrong to do that. Tilly told me that Dodie told her what happened with your bedroom. Told me what they thought." She stopped a moment, swallowing, then looked down at the teacup she still held. "I realize I was so wrong."

Cam heard the sorrow in her voice but layered through that was the thought of her callously discarding his memories. The things his mother had given him.

So he said nothing, waiting to see what else she would say.

She kept her eyes down. "I'm so, so sorry. I guess... I think I was just happy you were gone. I wanted to erase you out of my life and Dodie's. I knew Greg was foolish to let her go and so, when I found out that you had broken up with her, I told Greg not to be stupid. To go back to her. I thought they would come to live in this house, and I didn't want any reminder of you...so...so I cleaned it out. Threw it all away."

It made some kind of twisted sense, but it still hurt.

She looked up at him, tears drifting down her cheeks. "I was wrong. That's one reason I wanted you to come back to see me. I wanted to apologize to you for what I did. The past few years I've been attending a Bible study with Tilly and Dot and they've been helping me through this."

"Tilly helped you through this. I thought she hated me."

"Well, she had her own things to deal with. She and I are such dear friends, and we were so happy when Greg and Dodie started dating. I have to confess we kind of pushed them together, but they seemed happy. And then, when they got back together again...not as much."

"What do you mean?"

Kelly sighed. "Greg was gone a lot before he died. Took lots of trips. He told me he and Dodie should never have gotten married. That he didn't love her as much as he should. That he felt stressed and overwhelmed with her expectations. But I know Dodie and I love her and I know all she wants is her garden, greenhouse, and her woodworking shop. I know she would have loved to have children, but that didn't happen. She wasn't a demanding person."

Her words were like small cuts, but he sat and listened, letting her talk, thinking of the child Greg and Dodie had almost had.

"And I also know how much this farm meant to you. I should never have talked your father into letting me take it over."

This stunned Cam. "You were the one that made him change his will?"

"He didn't change much of it. Initially it was supposed to be me in charge until you turned twenty-one. I told him that this would tie my hands. I told him I would take care of you."

"But you didn't."

Kelly shook her head, lowering her gaze, saying nothing for a moment.

Cam struggled to stay quiet himself. To wait for her reasons.

Her excuses.

Her face was set in tight lines, her eyes narrowed. "I saw how your father doted on you and ignored Greg, and that wasn't right. Greg didn't think so either. He told me I had to make sure I was in charge so not everything would go to you. That I had rights too. He pushed me to make your father change the will. I thought it made sense."

Cam wanted to protest but again knew it would fall on deaf ears. Kelly also doted on her son. He could see Greg's intervention would have created tension between her and his father.

"I didn't think it was fair the way he talked about dividing it up," she continued, her words terse. "Half to you, one quarter to me, one quarter to Greg. So I told him it would be better if I got it all. And he finally agreed."

Once again Cam felt the sting of his father's capitulation. He wanted to ask how long it took for him to give in. If he fought for his own son.

He couldn't stop a wrench of anger and regret at what could have happened had Kelly not pushed his father. He could have stayed. He and Dodie could have been together.

Sucking in a deep breath, he sent up a prayer.

He had to leave that in the past.

Because if he found out his father had fought for him, he would be even more angry with Kelly. And if he hoped to live here, he would have to make his peace with her.

If his father had given in too quickly, however, it would tarnish the memory he had of a loving dad. What Kelly told him had already shifted those memories. Had filled the hole of sorrow he had felt after he found out about the will.

One step forward, one back, Cam thought as he listened to her justifications.

"But I'm taking over the farm now," Cam said, reminding himself to look ahead. To the future. "And I'm hoping we can make it work for both of us."

Kelly pressed her lips together as if to hold something more back from him. Then she nodded. "I hope so too." Another pause. "I'm sorry. I'm so sorry. I know what I did was wrong." She reached out to take his hand and, Lord forgive him, he wanted to pull his back. But he let her find her way through her regret.

"I want to make it up to you," she said. "And if you buy the farm, that could be a way."

"Let's just take it one step at a time, okay?" he said. Then he glanced at the clock. "I should get going. I squeezed in an appointment at the bank."

"Again, I'm so sorry."

Cam looked down at her, his anger shifting as he took in the tears glistening on her wrinkled cheeks. The sorrow in her eyes. *She's lost a husband and a son,* he reminded himself.

He nodded, then left.

"The letter you got dealt with missed loan payments," Jeff, the accounts manager sitting across the enormous desk, told him.

"Loan payments? On what?" Cam leaned forward, trying to get a glimpse of the computer screen Jeff had in front of him. "I know Greg bought a tractor, but the amount due in the letter is larger than that."

"Here, I'll show you."

CAROLYNE AARSEN

Jeff turned the computer screen so Cam could see the figures for himself.

"So here's where we have the outstanding loans." Jeff pulled his pen out of his pocket, using it to point out the very red lines on the balance sheet. "This one was taken out four years ago for the tractor. This other one, three years ago. A line of credit which was increased once, and the mortgage taken out on the property. We structured each of these loans for a once-a-year payment, due November first. I'm assuming this schedule was set up because of the timing of the sale of the calf crop and, of course, the harvest."

Cam's heart plunged as he looked at the numbers, confused. "There shouldn't be a mortgage on the farm," he said, frowning as the amount of the loans coalesced. "My dad inherited the place from his father and paid him out over time. I remember my dad being so proud of the fact that the only debt he had against the property was for the new tractor we had purchased. He didn't involve me in all the day-to-day financial actions, but I knew that there was very little debt incurred."

He rubbed his eyes as if that would change the numbers.

"So how far back do these financials go?" he asked.

Jeff slipped his glasses down his face and punched some dates into the computer, his fingers flying over the keyboard. The screen flashed a few times. Then he shook his head. "Our records only go back about four years. "I can dig deeper, but those are probably all archived. And there would be a fee attached to that."

Cam just rolled his eyes. "Of course there is a fee attached to me finding out about my own finances."

"If this was about your account, there wouldn't be. But because all of this is in Kelly's name, I have to charge you."

"Even though I gave you a letter from the lawyer, allowing me to act on her behalf."

"If it granted you power of attorney, there wouldn't be a fee."

"Fine. Do what you have to." Getting the history on the loans wouldn't change anything. It would just give him a better timeline of when the loans were taken out.

"Okay. I'll charge the amount to the bank account..." Jeff typed some more while Cam struggled with a mixture of confusion and anger. How could the farm have come to this? So much debt?

Jeff tapped the keyboard as the printer beside him spat out paper, each sheet twisting Cam's stomach tighter.

Jeff handed him the papers and Cam pulled his chair closer, looking over them as Jeff walked him through it.

" So if you look at the top, you've got the value of the land using estimates from the county. These are generally low, which of course works to your tax advantage, but they're not always realistic of the actual market. Right now the market is red hot. We do our own land evaluations based on what land has been selling for, and they skew higher."

Cam did some quick mental math, but as he looked at the column on the right, he knew there would not be much left when the farm sold.

"So how did you end up lending my brother so much money?" Cam asked as he took in the dates of the loans. All of them after his father died.

"One was an equipment purchase. We had value attached to that. The others were lines of credit we kept extending. One of those loans was satisfied when your mother-in-law sold the cows. I am sure she could have gotten more for the cows and paid some toward the line of credit, but I don't think she got good advice on that sale."

"Do you know how that happened?"

"Devon Collier made some kind of deal with her. He told her he would give her blanket cost for the cows, saving her the trouble of either running them to the auction mark or having a farm sale. I believe..." He looked down at the paper then up at the computer screen, tapping his pencil against his lips. "I believe this is a couple months after the unfortunate passing of your brother. She came to us after the fact, and while how she handled this frustrated me, this was well after the fact, and I couldn't change anything."

"So you're saying she could have gotten more money for the cows?" It had been a substantial herd. When he left, there were at least one hundred and fifty pure-bred Angus cows and calves.

"Yes, she could have."

Cam's anger was like a stone in his gut. One more reason to fire Devon Collier and not let him touch anything connected to the farm.

But the bigger question was, how could his brother have amassed so much debt in only four years? And what was it for? "How did you let him get away with all this?" The question burst out of him, anger on its heels.

Jeff shrugged, giving him a sympathetic look. "This was before my time. By the time I got the account the damage had been done and your brother had passed on. We assumed that he had taken out a life insurance policy to cover the indebtedness, but it wasn't as large as it should have been and of course that went to his wife. She wasn't a part of the farm, so therefore we couldn't touch it."

All this evading of responsibility fed his anger. He had to force himself to unclench his fists. To lower his shoulders.

"Did Dodie know about any of this?"

"That I'm not aware of. Everything here was taken out in Greg's name, so I'm not sure."

He couldn't believe that she would have taken part in this. He wondered what she knew about it.

"So who was his accounts manager before you?"

"Some guy named Paul Decovil."

Greg's old friend and drinking buddy. Obviously Paul had gotten his act together enough to at least get a job in the bank. Helping Greg borrow money.

"I heard that Greg's mother, Kelly, is thinking of selling the farm," Jeff continued.

Cam shouldn't be surprised. In Millars Crossing everyone knew everyone else's business.

"It's a good market right now," Jeff said. "You'll easily cover the loans and have some left over."

"And if we didn't sell?"

Jeff pursed his lips, tapping his pen on his chin. "You'll have to come up with enough to satisfy the loan payments and the interest accrued."

"And with the cattle gone, the income would be vastly reduced."

"Unless you decide to purchase them again."

"Which would mean another loan." Cam pressed the palms of his hands to his eyes, hoping to stave off the headache he could feel blossoming behind his eyes.

"Or you could bundle the loans and we could set up a payment schedule. There's room."

Cam couldn't think right now.

"I'll have to get back to you," he said, feeling the pinch of time speeding up. In two weeks he had to be in Vancouver and a couple of weeks after that they were headed out for their first gig in Seattle.

"You've got all you need there," Jeff said, pointing to the sheaf of papers Cam had laid out in front of him.

"I do. I have to see the accountant next, so I imagine he'll have more bad news for me."

Jeff gave him a sympathetic smile as they both stood. "I'm sorry I couldn't be the bearer of better news. I hope you get things sorted out."

"Me too," Cam muttered, giving him a forced smile as he shook his hand.

But as he strode out of the office, clenching the papers, Cam struggled with the anger that was now boiling.

However, what cut him the deepest, what swept the ground out from under his feet, was the reality that even the tiny notion he had entertained of buying Kelly out and taking over the farm had been wiped out with each page that printer spat out.

CHAPTER THIRTEEN

*C*am looked over stacks of papers and statements he'd gotten from the accountant and the accounts manager. He had set them out on the table in the AirBnB he was staying at in chronological order. This was the fifth or sixth time, maybe more, he had gone over them.

Nothing had changed.

His hands clenched into fists as he processed the figures once again. Numbers had never been his strong suit, but even he could tell that the farm, once prosperous and thriving, had descended into a morass of debt and unpaid credit cards. He glanced over the statements, his anger growing with each transaction.

It seemed his brother had a fondness for trips to Vegas. Very expensive fondness. Had racked up bills, increased the credit limit on three credit cards.

Operating loans had been used to the maximum, lines of credit had been applied for and received by Greg's good

CAROLYNE AARSEN

friend Paul Decovil to pay off the credit cards. It was just a
matter of some simple addition and subtraction to see the
farm that was once worth well into the millions was deeply
indebted and worth much less.

And he guessed that was why Kelly was vacating it now.
Selling it before more of the capital was eaten up by interest
rates.

How much did Kelly know about this?

Had she known that her beloved son, the bright shining
star in her life, had turned out to be a ball of fiery
destruction?

Cam's stomach twisted at what he saw. How could the
farm that he and his father had poured so much of themselves into end up in such bad financial shape?

The amount he had saved up would be enough to pay
down the credit card debt with some left over for operating
capital to purchase cows. But not enough for a down
payment on what the farm was truly worth on the market.
He needed more cash.

But where to get it?

His mind was a world of anger and confusion and
sorrow.

His thoughts slipped to Dodie. The plan he had hoped to
put into place for their future. Together.

He and Kelly needed to talk. He had to make some kind
of deal with her that didn't include him buying the farm
from her. It would mean her dream of purchasing a house in
town would have to change. If she wanted to move to Millars
Crossing, she would have to live in an apartment.

Once she found out what Greg had done, he hoped she
wouldn't be pressing her "rights," insisting on her dream of a
new home in town.

And his dreams?

He had indulged in a few last night after he and Dodie had talked.

After singing in church.

Building a studio on the farm. A place he could write his own songs, possibly record a solo album. He had enough connections, he knew he could pull it together. But there wouldn't be enough money to do it. What he had thought of as a decent investment for his own future now drowned in a sea of red ink.

The money from the world tour could save them.

The thought stuck in his mind, twisted his gut.

Going on that tour would mean leaving for a year on top of being gone six months. That would put his time away from Dodie at over a year and a half.

Which meant he was back to where he had been when he and Dodie broke up in the first place.

He knew then how connected she was to home and family. Her little oasis and her work. He knew how important that was to her. Her desire for home and family would be beaten down by the demands of steady travel, staying in different places every few days, and constantly meeting new people. Could their love survive this?

He leaned back in his chair and dragged his hands over his face, sending up an anguished prayer.

Dear Lord, I don't know how to see my way through this. I don't want to lose Dodie again. But it looks like that might happen.

And the worst part of it was, this time, he knew, it would hurt far worse than the last time.

DODIE LOOKED out the window of the farmhouse just as Cam's truck pulled up.

And her heart gave another flare of anticipation.

Yesterday after he left she couldn't sleep, she was so happy. So excited.

So instead, she made plans. Tried to decide what to do when Cam was back from touring. Where they would live.

She hoped he would be willing to stay in her little house. She had put so much work into the cabin and the yard. It was her home, and she hoped Cam would be okay with making it his home too, despite Greg having once lived here.

The farmhouse was nice, but it never felt like home the way her cabin and surrounding yard did.

Cam stayed in the truck, talking on the phone. Even from here she could see he wasn't happy.

After a short while, he got out of the truck. Instead of coming directly up the walk, however, he stood by his truck, hands on his hips, looking over the yard, and to the mountains beyond. He plowed his hand through his hair and then marched up the walk. He disappeared, and the door opened and slammed shut.

The sound echoed in the silence, startling Dodie.

What was going on?

No sooner had the question formed than Cam stormed into the kitchen. His hair was disheveled, his eyes narrowed, and his jaw clenched with what looked like anger.

He looked at her and for a moment she thought she had done something wrong.

Then she lifted her chin, reminding herself that Cam wasn't Greg.

Of course Greg hadn't been Greg the last year of their marriage. Surly, angry, easily upset. She often asked if he wanted to talk about it, but he always waved her off. Saying it was his problem, he would solve it.

"Where's Kelly?" Cam ground out, shaking off his jacket

and setting it on the deacon bench just inside the door leading to the entrance.

"She made it up the stairs this afternoon and is sitting in her bedroom."

Dodie had been encouraging Kelly to take a few steps up and down the stairs as part of her daily physical therapy. Reminding her that the better her mobility, the sooner she could move to town. Thankfully Kelly took her advice to heart and now could go all the way up to her room.

"Excellent. I need to talk to her private."

Dodie wiped her hands on the cloth she had just used to clean the counters and turned to watch as he strode across the kitchen and then took the stairs two at a time.

She swallowed down her fears, reminding herself that it was all well. She and Cam had plans. They were going to be married and live in Millars Crossing.

And this time nothing was stopping that from happening.

With this in mind, she set the lasagna someone had brought in the oven and then moved into the living room. She took the sheets off of Kelly's bed and changed them out for clean ones. Tidied up a little. Fluffed the pillows.

Fussy busy work.

She had taken the time to visit Kelly this afternoon because she was getting ahead on the canoes. Cam told her he would help her again this evening, and she hoped he would try out the guitar again. The thought made her smile.

She sat down on the couch and pulled out her iPad. She had an idea for another guitar she wanted to make for Cam. This one would have an inlaid design that would be tricky. She didn't want it to affect the sound.

However, as she sketched and experimented with patterns, the rising and falling murmur of conversation above her snagged her attention. Cam had closed the door. Whatever it was he had to talk to Kelly about, it must be serious. When Cam told her he was heading to town to talk to the bank and the lawyer, she felt a thrill of excitement. He was following through on their plans. And she guessed his conversation with Kelly had something to do with those very plans.

Now Dodie's ears perked up as the conversation grew louder. Cam sounded angry, but so did Kelly.

This couldn't be good for Kelly. Dodie set her iPad aside, was about to stand, then hesitated.

Her mind zipped to the empty room Kelly had stripped of everything that had once been Cam's. She'd had no right to interfere in their history.

Seeing that room had been a huge turning point for her. It made her see Kelly in a different light.

See her through Cam's eyes, not Greg's.

As the voices grew in intensity, she grew more concerned. It bothered her deeply that two people she cared for sounded so at odds with each other.

She walked up the stairs and knocked on the door.

"Come in."

"Please stay away," Cam said simultaneously.

Dodie laid her hand against the door, not sure who to listen to. However, curiosity and fear made her turn the knob and step into the room. Cam stood by the window, his hands planted on his hips, legs spread, his back to her as he looked out the window. An aggressive stance if she ever saw one.

Kelly sat in a chair in one corner of her room, chin up, lips pressed together.

"This might be none of my business, but I am feeling a little concerned. Kelly's only been out of the hospital a couple of weeks–"

"Please. Not now." Cam held up one hand as if to stop her.

Dodie glanced over at Kelly, whose eyes glistened with

tears. When she blinked, one slipped down her cheek and she reached up to wipe it away. She swallowed, clearly distressed.

"Can someone tell me what's happening?" Dodie asked, glancing over at Cam who was clutching the back of his neck with one hand, still standing with his back to the room.

"Cam has been making some horrible accusations about my son, your husband, Greg. About things I have no control over."

"What kind of accusations?" Dodie looked from Cam to Kelly, but neither of them would look at her.

She waited a beat and then, finally, Cam spun around.

The anguish on his face shocked her. Especially after hearing his voice raised to Kelly just a few moments ago.

She hurried to his side, placing her hand on his arm. "What's the matter?"

Cam's eyes held a sorrow that baffled and frightened her at the same time.

"I just found out how bad the farm's financial situation is," he said, his voice tense, hard.

"What do you mean?"

Cam lifted his hand and stroked her cheek, his eyes following the movements of his fingers. "I don't want to talk about it, not really."

"Doesn't matter," she said, catching his hand and gripping it. "You and I are getting married. You need to tell me."

Kelly's swift intake of breath showed Dodie what impact her proclamation had on her mother-in-law, but right now Dodie didn't care. At all.

Cam rubbed his fingers over his forehead, closing his eyes a moment. Then he looked down at her, his eyes sorrowful. "I can't buy the farm the way it is. I can't afford it with the money I have."

"But you'll make money from the tour," she said, trying to keep up with the words he was throwing out.

Can't buy.

Can't afford.

"I will, but there are too many debts against the farm."

"Debts? What debts? How?" She shot a look toward Kelly. "I thought you paid them off when you sold the cows."

But Kelly wasn't looking at her. Instead she was worrying with a button on her cardigan, lips pressed together. So she turned back to Cam. "Tell me about these debts?"

Another sigh from Cam.

"Tell me," she insisted, giving his arm a shake.

Cam swallowed, then met her gaze again. "Greg was gambling the year before he died. Hard. He and his buddy Paul would go to Vegas and play poker. With the high rollers. He used collateral from the farm to shore up his losses. And he lost big."

"How big?"

"Hundreds of thousands big."

The muscles in her neck seized up, her throat closed off as a wall of panic slammed into her at his words.

She struggled to breathe, her hands still clutching Cam's arm in a death grip.

"Hundreds? Of thousands?" She could only manage those words as what Cam said dropped into her soul. And then, behind that, came a wave of anger and shame. "He used to tell me he only went there to blow off steam. To relax. To just play some slots, some blackjack. And now you're telling me he was playing high-stakes poker?" How could she have not known? She should have stopped him.

Cam's expression grew sympathetic. "I'm so sorry, Dodie. I know what he meant to you."

Yes, he had meant a lot to her. She had always cared for him. They had dated for years before they got married.

Despite the feelings for Cam that she had worked so hard to suppress, she and Greg had found some measure of happiness.

Until the last year.

And suddenly everything became clear to her. "That's why he was so angry all the time," she breathed, ice slithering through her veins. "He was so snappy and frustrated. Then he would pull out of it, apologize, and take me out for dinner. Buy me some flowers." She released a harsh laugh. "Hoping to make it up to me."

She shot a pleading look at Cam. "I didn't know it had gotten so bad. None. No idea that he was gambling this badly." She stopped, realizing how desperate she sounded, but it was important that Cam knew she had nothing to do with it all.

"Dodie wasn't involved with the finances," Kelly put in, her words a surprising defense. "Don't be angry with her."

Cam shook his head and pulled Dodie into a gentle embrace. "I'm not angry with you at all," he said, stroking her hair, pressing a kiss on the top of her head. "I believe you. I know you would let nothing jeopardize the farm." His chest rose and fell on a deep sigh, and in it she heard resignation and worry.

She pulled back, looking up at him. "So, what do we do? How can we work our way out of this? I will help however I can."

His smile was gentle, but in it she saw the futility of her offer. How many canoes or guitars would she have to build to put even the smallest dent in that much money? Hundreds and hundreds.

"I have to talk to the banker again, but we need to change some plans."

Dread crawled up her throat.

"How so?" was all she could choke out.

Cam plunged his hand through his hair. "I'll have to take that European tour. On top of the North American one. It's the only way I can generate enough cash to get the farm back on its feet again." He looked over at Kelly, frustration crossing his features, then fading. "And Kelly has agreed that I won't be purchasing the farm from her. Instead, I will furnish her with a yearly income instead of what she would get after the sale of the farm."

His words spun around Dodie's head as he continued talking about equity, re-financing, debt consolidation. How it could work if he could get the bank to cooperate now that Kelly was on board.

But all the time he spoke the only words echoing through her head were *six months. One year.* They had just found each other again and he would have to leave again for over a year and a half.

How could she bear it?

"There's no other way?" she asked, realizing how harshly her words came out.

Another gentle smile, another touch of his hand on her shoulder, and then a shake of his head. "I went over and over the numbers. Talked to Finn and Wyatt. Ran some ideas past them. It will all work, but I'll need the cash from the tours in order to get the farm going."

Dodie swallowed down her sorrow, her eyes fixed on him.

"It's okay," he assured her. "I'll sneak away and come and visit when I can."

"But you'll be so far away," was all she could say.

"And when it's over, we'll get married and we'll be together for the rest of our lives."

He sounded so casual about it, but the lines of tension around his mouth showed her the toll this decision had taken on him.

"But let's not talk about that now," he said. "I want to take you out for dinner and then go out for another canoe ride. See the loons."

"And when do you have to leave for Vancouver?"

He emitted another sigh. "Because of the extra work going over the plans for the world tour, I have to leave on Friday."

"That's only four days away," she cried.

"But it will be a good four days," he said with a rueful smile. "I'm back in Edmonton for a quick gig on Friday. We could see each other then."

"I have an appointment in Regina then. For another contract." And if he was gone that long, she would need to keep herself busy. She would need the work.

She wanted to be strong, wanted to remind herself that people had been separated longer than she would be from Cam.

But it still hurt.

And, what made it worse, was all of this was because of the actions of his stepbrother. Kelly's son.

Her husband.

Why hadn't she seen? Why hadn't she paid more attention?

"It's not your fault," Cam said, as if he could read her mind.

"But I should have known." She turned to Kelly and fought the urge to toss her frustration in her lap.

But Kelly was crying, looking down, not meeting either of their eyes.

What good would it do to be angry? It would solve nothing.

"We should make sure you get back downstairs, Kelly," was all she could manage for now. "I put supper in the oven. I know you can fend for yourself. I'll be back later to say goodnight."

Kelly shook her head. "I'll be okay. I have my phone. If I need any help, I'll phone your mom."

Part of her wanted to object, but another part of her didn't want to waste any of her precious time left with Cam.

So she just nodded and left, Cam following along behind her.

CHAPTER FOURTEEN

"I'll miss the quiet," Cam said as they tied the canoe up to the dock.

The past few days had been idyllic, despite the noise of working in the shop. Being with Dodie had made every whine of the sander, every smell of the resin and itch of the fiberglass worthwhile.

Dodie said nothing as she got out of the canoe, and Cam suspected she was crying. Tomorrow morning, early, he had to leave. He was saying goodbye to her here.

Now.

He wanted to do this in a quiet place, away from people. In her little paradise that she treasured so dearly.

They had talked endlessly about Greg and Kelly and the farm's situation until Cam put an end to the conversations. It got them nowhere, and he wanted Dodie to keep more good memories of Greg than bad.

As did he. Anger only sucked what precious joy he had of

being with Dodie this last day together. He preferred to talk about their future, not the past.

"I'll miss you," Dodie returned as she got out behind Cam.

"Well, that's good to know." Cam picked up the paddles, laid them on his shoulder, and grabbed Dodie's hand as they walked down the dock. "I'll miss you too."

"All those adoring fans won't make you forget me?"

Cam knew she was teasing, but he also heard the faintest note of concern in her voice. He stopped, turning to her, shaking his head. "The guy those girls are screaming at is not me. It's who I pretend to be. The only person who knows the true me is you."

He could see Dodie swallow, as if holding back another comment.

He brushed a gentle kiss over her lips, his hand cupping her face, his thumb gently tracing her mouth when he pulled back. "I am going to miss you like crazy."

Deep in the depths of his soul, a question simmered.

Come with me.

But he pushed that down.

He didn't want to leave this place. He couldn't imagine that she would. Besides, all he could offer her were hotel rooms, eating takeout, and moving from place to place. Busyness, noise, and endless rehearsals.

"I'll miss you too," she said, her voice choked. "Do you have to go so soon?"

"I'm meeting my manager in Calgary and we have to go over a few things before we get together with the band. He wanted to take care of it as soon as possible."

"Remember, you'll be able to see wherever I am on your phone, and I'm only a text, FaceTime or call away."

They had agreed to follow each other with what Dodie jokingly called a "stalker app." It was a simple app that allowed her to see where he was whenever his phone was on and vice versa. Another way to stay connected.

"It will be painful to see you all the way in California while I'm up here in Alberta," she grumbled. "Seeing all that space between us."

"We'll FaceTime when I can," he promised her, hating that they were making these arrangements while they were walking toward her cabin.

He released her hand when they came to the path, and she went on ahead. He watched her from behind, his heart aching with the pain of the goodbye they had to say in a few moments.

"Just put the paddles on the deck, beside the swing," Dodie said, shooting him a quick glance over her shoulder. "I have to get something for you. Don't go away."

A goodbye present, he was pretty sure.

But when she came out of the house carrying a guitar case, then knelt down and pulled out a gleaming guitar, his heart folded in his chest.

"I made a strap for it," she said, fingering the colorful band. "I embroidered my name in it and yours. Just to remind you."

As if he needed a reminder of her. He had photos galore and her face was on his screen whenever his phone was on.

"That's amazing," he breathed, taking the guitar from her, running his hands over its shining surface. It seemed too beautiful to take on tour.

"I know it's not near the caliber of your Taylor or your Martin, but it was made with love, so that has to help."

"When did you manage to do this?" They had spent so much time together.

"A lot of late nights."

He took it reverently from her, slipped the strap over his shoulder. He strummed it, adjusted one of the tuning pegs,

CAROLYNE AARSEN

strummed again, then felt a blend of sorrow and gratitude flow through him.

"It sounds rich and full and has a beautiful shimmer." He played a C chord then an A minor, slipping into a G. "I know most guys like C, F, and G, but I love the minor chord." As he played, he gave her a pensive smile. "Three chords and the truth," he said, quoting an old country music saying. And as the sound resonated in the yard, he felt the tug of the yearning to sing. To perform. That dichotomy between knowing he would be alone, knowing the hard times ahead, and yet the rush he got from hearing people singing along to the songs he wrote.

This tour was supposed to be his last, but now he would be on the road for over a year and a half.

And as he looked at Dodie, who was smiling even as tears slid down her cheeks, he knew this tour would be one of the hardest ones. One that would tear at his soul.

But one he would have to do if he wanted a future with Dodie.

Here, in Millars Crossing.

He finished strumming, took the guitar off and, still holding it, gave Dodie a one-armed hug, pulling her tight against him.

"Thanks, Dodie. This is the best gift I've ever gotten. I'll use it in my performances."

"You don't have to," she protested, leaning back, her hands on his chest, "But I wanted you to have it before you left."

"I know I don't have to, but it's beautiful. You did an amazing job for your second guitar."

"I wish," she said with a chuckle. "There's a lot of guitar bodies that went up in smoke before I finished this one."

He gave her another kiss and then, though it pained him, he glanced at his watch. He sucked in a deep breath, put the guitar carefully back in the case. Snapped it up, then stood.

"Sorry, babe. I gotta go."

She grinned at the old term he used to use for her. "Of course." She held him once more, then turned and picked up the guitar case. It carried well. The heft and weight so familiar.

Another long look, another kiss.

And with tears in both their eyes this time, he turned and walked toward his truck. He set the guitar carefully inside, then got in himself. He wished he could just drive away, but he looked back to see Dodie, one hand covering her mouth, the other waving.

He waved back, started his truck, and before he could change his mind, chuck everything, and go back to her, he reversed out of the spot and drove away.

He watched Dodie grow smaller until a bend in the driveway hid her from view.

And he fought down anguished tears all the way to Calgary.

"THIS LOOKS COZY," Dodie said, looking around the apartment. The living room window overlooked downtown Millars Crossing and from the dining room, Kelly could see the faintest view of the mountains.

"I think I'll be happy here," Kelly said from her recliner by the window.

They had moved in all her furniture, at least what could fit. The rest had joined the boxes in the shed.

Finn, Wyatt, Reuben, and Luke, Janie's husband, had all come to help Kelly move in. They had just left and now Dodie and Kelly were here alone.

The day Cam left, Kelly decided she didn't want to stay on the ranch a minute longer than she had. Dodie and Janie found her this apartment on short notice and she liked it.

Deal was done, the lease was signed, and she moved in the next day.

As they emptied the house, Dodie felt a surge of melancholy. She had so many memories here. She had to remind herself that she and Cam would make more.

Someday she told herself. Meantime, she was working with another company to build more custom canoes. She hadn't signed anything yet, but the work would keep her busy for at least four months with an option of building for them full-time. Which had its plusses and minuses. Though she loved building canoes, she wasn't sure she wanted to do it day after day.

But what else was she supposed to do for a year and a half?

"So where is Cam now?" Kelly asked, easing back into her chair.

She looked tired, and Dodie couldn't blame her. Though she didn't have to do any of the physical work, she'd had to make a lot of decisions about what she wanted where.

"He's in Vancouver last I checked. But he's flying back to Edmonton to do an opening act for a friend. As a favor. Then he's back to Vancouver."

"When will that be happening?"

"Tomorrow," Dodie said.

"Are you driving up to see him?"

Dodie bit her lip and shook her head. "I'm meeting the head of the canoe company in Regina tomorrow afternoon."

She had checked the distance, just to see if she could run up to Edmonton to see Cam, but it was an eight-hour drive one way. She wouldn't arrive in Edmonton until two o'clock in the morning, and Cam had said he was flying out right after the gig.

So, that was a no.

It was the closest he would be for the next six months.

Again she sent up another prayer, reminding herself that they would see each other between the tours. She would just have to be patient. At least this time around she knew why he was leaving.

And that he would be back.

"I got a call from someone who wanted to buy the farm," Kelly said, giving Dodie a tight smile. "I told him it wasn't for sale."

Dodie nodded then plumped up some pillows and straightened a picture. She'd told Janie she would be available in twenty minutes to help out in the Corner Café while Janie took her daughter to the dentist. Her other helper was off sick, so Dodie said she would fill in.

Something to do.

"Then he asked if we would be willing to sell your place. Said to name your price, he loved it so much."

Dodie gave Kelly a hard frown. "I hope you told him no."

"I did. But he left his name and number and said if you ever change your mind."

As if that would happen. Her acreage was her sanctuary. And with Cam gone, it would be even more so.

"Not interested," Dodie said with finality.

She was just ready to leave when Kelly cleared her throat.

"Dodie," she said, looking over at her, "I don't know if I ever said it, but I'm so thankful for all your help these past weeks. It's been such a comfort to have you around."

Dodie gave her a cautious smile, still unable to erase the anger that often overcame her. It was because of Kelly's pampering of Greg, her enabling, that Cam couldn't be back here for over a year and a half. That they had to be separated again.

"And I have something else to say," Kelly continued. "I know it's too little too late, but I am so, so sorry about what Greg did. I should have stopped him. I should have said no whenever he wanted to borrow more money."

"Yes, you should have." The words burst out before Dodie could stop them. Ever since she found out what Greg had done her emotions veered between anger with him and anger with his mother and sometimes both.

"In my defense, I never knew how bad it was getting." Kelly gave her a beseeching look, and for a moment Dodie felt her pain. But just a moment.

"So you never looked at the books at all?" Dodie asked.

Kelly gave a careful shrug. "Even with Cam's father, I had no idea of the finances. I was raised that it wasn't important that a woman know. That her husband was responsible for that."

Dodie was tired. Tired of being angry. Maintaining a grudge was a lot of work.

This is more than a grudge.

Dodie dismissed the thought. Kelly would be around for a while, and sooner or later Dodie had to find some measure of peace. It would be easier if she did it sooner rather than later.

"I'm sorry you weren't involved more as well," Dodie said. "But neither was I, and I was Greg's wife and supposed partner."

"But it wasn't your farm," Kelly said, defending her.

"No, but I was more than willing to have my living paid for by that farm." She gave Kelly a careful smile. "And maybe I should have been more involved."

Kelly shook her head. "Please don't take any of this on. It's all me. And even if you were involved, do you think you could've stopped Greg?"

Dodie thought back to the last year of their marriage. The anger that always hung over Greg like a dark cloud. How he would snap at her. And then apologize.

"No, probably not," she admitted.

"And I'm so sorry... I keep saying this... But I am. I can't apologize enough for what this has created for you and Cam. That you have to be separated so long while he tries to make enough money to set himself up on the farm. Please forgive me."

"I'm sorry too," Dodie said. "And I forgive you. I can't stay angry about this. I have to move on."

"Like I said, I never deserved you. I tried so hard to get you and Greg to date, but that was because I knew what a good person you were." She twisted her hands, looking down. "But I have to say you are always happiest when you were with Cam. You two looked like you belong together. Acted like you belong together. I wanted the same thing, that deep connection, for my son and you. I'm sorry that your mother and I pushed you two so hard together after Cam left."

Her words created a small twinge of guilt. But Dodie brushed that aside. She was tired of looking back with regret. "You need to know that Greg and I had happy times. I loved him and I know he loved me. But I'm looking forward to when Cam and I can be with each other again."

"I just wish it wouldn't have to take so long," Kelly said with genuine sorrow in her voice.

"So do I," Dodie said. "Sometimes I wish we would've gotten married before he left. Then at least I could've called my husband instead of my boyfriend while he's gone."

"Too bad you two didn't elope."

Dodie had to laugh at that.

Kelly looked up, holding her gaze, Her eyes intent. "If you're worried about how he'll behave on the tour... I don't think you need to. He loves you dearly and deeply. I know that for a fact. I know there are temptations for him on the road, but I also know he loves you too much to give into any of that. He is a man of deep integrity. That much I know as well."

Dodie gave her a smile and glanced at her watch again. "I should get going."

She brushed a gentle kiss over Kelly's forehead, then left, smiling at what her mother-in-law had said.

As she drove to her sister's café, a strange and erratic idea spun around the back of her mind.

She tried to dismiss it, but it wouldn't leave.

However, as soon as she stepped into the busy noisiness of her sister's café, it was pushed down.

But during every lull, and then as she cleaned up afterward, it grew and morphed. The more space she gave it, the more she embraced it.

CHAPTER FIFTEEN

"**I**'m stoked you agreed to doing the world tour," Gage said, tapping out more information on his ever-present iPad.

Cam sat on the bed of the hotel in Edmonton, legs stretched out in front of him, his guitar on his lap as he picked out a song.

"It's fantastic exposure. The logistics will be a challenge, but we've got half a year to work that out and we can fiddle with the schedule as we go," Gage continued. "We can do some on the fly. I've got enough connections to help me with booking the venues."

Gage frowned as he tapped a few more things out, either not noticing or caring that Cam had said nothing. "And while I theoretically have your attention, are you okay with doing some smaller gigs on the side? Let's say a pub or a bar?"

Cam looked up from playing Dodie's guitar, trying to

drum up some enthusiasm. "Sure. We could do that. I don't mind busy. But remember what I said."

"Gotcha. You're not sharing a room." Gage leaned back in the office chair of the hotel, his hands behind his head. "I know I shouldn't push you too hard on this, but after the world tour, what do you say to doing some recording sessions?"

Cam didn't want to think any further than the next gig. Let alone that far in the future.

"I can book a sound studio down in Calgary. You can come up from your farm and do some work from time to time."

It was his words, "come up from your farm" that created a tiny sliver of hope and expectation.

Cam strummed a few more chords, smiling at the rich tone coming from the guitar. A guitar that every time he picked it up would make him think of Dodie.

"I don't know if I want to take it that far yet. But it's worth keeping in mind. I'd love to write some more songs, spend some time in one place."

"Running cattle and planting crops should give you lots of inspiration." Gage laughed.

That was so far in the future Cam couldn't allow himself to go there. *Just do what comes next*, he reminded himself.

Gage pushed to his feet. "Well, I've got a plane to catch, and you've got a gig to practice for. When do you have to head out to Rexall Place?"

"I've got at least six hours," Cam said.

"You can explore Edmonton while you're waiting," Gage said with a chuckle. He dropped his iPad into his case, which he slung over his shoulder. "Don't get lost and I'll see you back in Vancouver," he said with a wave of his hand.

And then he was gone.

Cam laid his guitar down on the bed and walked to the

window. He had booked a hotel close to the center so he could leave as soon as possible and then head to the airport and wait for his flight.

Cam pushed his fingers through his hair and blew out a sigh as he looked out the window over the city streets below him. He had come in last night and for a moment had toyed with the idea of going down to Millars Crossing. Seeing Dodie one more time.

But he knew she had to go to Regina today.

Trouble was, he had at least five hours to kill. The thought of sitting in the hotel room depressed him.

He walked over to the closet, opened it, and pulled out a denim jacket. Faded and worn, it was one he'd had for years.

A sudden knock on the door startled him. Gage probably forgot something.

He opened the door, ready to razz him about it when his mouth dropped open in shock.

Dodie stood in front of him, her eyes bright, wearing a white shirt tucked into blue jeans. Her hair was pulled back with a few flowers woven in. And was that glitter in her hair? Didn't matter, she looked gorgeous.

"Hey, babe, what... How..." He dragged his scattered thoughts together. "I thought you were supposed to be in Regina?"

He pulled her into the hotel room, closed the door, and planted a hard, warm kiss on her lips.

It was all he could do.

"I have better things to do," she said when he pulled away. "Are you busy right now?"

"I was just heading out to walk around the city." He ran his hands up and down her arms, trying to absorb the fact that she was here. With him.

She nodded, her expression a blend of mischief and a

vague shyness. "There's a place a couple blocks from here I want to go to with you."

"Sure... Of course..." He pulled her close in a tight hug. "I can't believe you came here. I can't believe you canceled your plans."

"Well, I might affect your plans a little."

He frowned, confused as to what was going on, yet so thrilled to see her.

"Grab your wallet and your passport," she said. "We need all the ID you can get."

"I'm old enough to drink," he said, taking refuge in teasing, her comment puzzling him even more. What was going on?

"Yeah, and you're old enough to get married too."

"Well, yeah." His thoughts spun around as he tried to follow her confusing lead.

"And I'm not waiting a year and a half for that to happen. I made an appointment at a registry's office a couple blocks down the street, and then you and I are meeting Janie and Luke and Pastor Simons. In a park overlooking the river. And we're getting married."

All Cam could do was stare at her.

"What are you talking about? What's going on?"

Dodie's expression grew serious as she placed her hands on his chest, her eyes clinging to his. "I don't want you to go on tour without me. I'm coming with you. But I'm coming as your wife. So that means we need to get married right away while you're still in Alberta."

"But...your place...your work..." He didn't know what to say first, how to absorb what she was telling him.

"Yeah. I know," she admitted, tracing his lips with her finger, sending shivers scooting down his spine. "Yes, I will miss my cabin and I will miss my home, but I miss you more. I'm putting it up for sale."

"You're not."

"I am. The money is paying down some of the farm debts. I got top dollar for it. My wedding present to you. Because we are getting married and I'm not letting you go away for eighteen months without me."

"Wedding present?"

She grinned, waving her hand in front of his face. "Catch up, please. I need you with me on this."

"I'm ....I'm trying...I still can't believe you're here." He held her eyes, shaking his head in amazement. "You want to get married now? Sell your place? Are you sure?"

"As sure as I've ever been," she said, her tone holding an edge he'd never heard before. A don't-mess-with-me vibe was rolling off her. "And I know this is a shock, but this is happening."

"You coming on the tour with me as well? I just..."

She held her hand up. "Don't give me some song and dance about not being able to give me what I want. Because right now the only thing I want is you. Nothing else. I don't care about my tomatoes, my gladiolas, my dahlias, pansies, cosmos, or my canoes or my loons or my lake. I don't care about any of that. I mean, I do, but you know, I just...I just..."

Like a deflated balloon she dropped on his bed, her hands resting on her lap, staring up at him.

"I've got everything planned, and you know I hate changing my plans," she finished.

Again Cam struggled to wrap his head around all this. "So we're doing this wedding thing right away?"

She waved her hand over her white shirt and pointed to her hair. "This is my wedding outfit and my wedding hair. So, yeah." Then her expression shifted. "Unless you're changing your mind again."

She was really serious about this.

"Of course I want to be married to you more than anything, but don't you want something...more...substantial?"

"I had substantial. Trust me. Between Kelly and Tilly and my sister I got dragged into a wedding that was a cross between *Keeping up with the Kardashians* and Martha Stewart. My dress was the most uncomfortable thing I'd ever worn. This, however, is epically comfortable. And Janie has the flowers. We just need the license."

Cam shook his head. "So you'd come with me on my tours?"

"Yeah. I figure I'll be able to see countries I've never seen before. It will be an adventure." Then her expression grew serious. "And I want to do it with you. Do you understand? You look confused."

"I'm stunned. I'm flabbergasted. I've never done this before."

"This is a first for me too," she said. "Now, kiss me again, because you need to practice for when we do our vows."

Again, Cam was at a loss for words. Dodie was like a force to be reckoned with and obviously determined to do this. But he knew that suddenly, miraculously, the next year and a half had gained a whole new luster. A new appeal.

He looked down at Dodie, pulled her to her feet, and did exactly what she wanted, his heart banging against his ribs so hard he thought it would burst out.

He pulled back, and she was smiling up at him, looking pretty self-satisfied. Then he caught a glimmer of uncertainty and he had to smile.

"You have just made me the happiest man in the world," he said, kissing her again.

She released a sigh and her smile softened. "That's always a good thing."

"So, this registry place. I'm assuming you googled it?"

She held up her phone. "I have it on the maps app. Just down the street."

"Excellent." Then just before they were ready to walk out the door, he stopped. "I don't have a ring for you."

"Relax," she said. "There's a jewelry store right beside the registry office."

"You really do have this all planned."

"I had a bit of time to organize it," she said, giving him a smile that made his heart shiver. "It kept me sane while I dithered and wondered if I could pull it off."

"I'd say you've done a masterful job. So, my next question is, white gold or regular gold?"

She laughed and swatted him gently. Then she grabbed her purse. "Get your stuff, we need to get going."

He did as he was told and then, arm in arm, they walked out of the hotel room.

As they left the building, Cam took a moment to look over at her.

"What are you thinking?" she asked.

"That this would make a great country song."

She laughed and together, they walked down the street and into their future.

THE LAST CHORDS of the final song rang through the arena, then the crowd, silent for a moment, burst into applause that filled the space, echoed off the walls.

Cam lifted his cowboy hat in a gesture of thanks as the thundering applause rolled over him and the band.

It was exhilarating and satisfying and, at the same time, exhausting.

Strobe lights flashed over the audience. Cell phone screens glittered back at him and as he turned, he caught

Dodie sitting on the scaffolding, head resting on one of the crossbars, watching him, her smile almost breaking her face.

Carefully, cautiously, she eased herself off the contraption.

Gage was there to help her down, and as she came to the bottom, she arched her back, running her hand over the small bulge of her stomach.

Cam waved again to the crowd in Hamburg who were now stomping their feet, calling out for another song.

It had been their third encore, and he wanted nothing more than to go back to the hotel and soak in the Jacuzzi.

With his wife and unborn child.

Then he gave in to an impulse and waved Dodie over.

He leaned into the mike.

"Folks, Hamburg is Sons of the Homesteaders last stop of the tour, and I thought it fitting to introduce you to my wife, Frau Dodie Morgan."

Laughter and cheering erupted as Dodie, blinking against the bright lights, walked slowly across the stage, careful to avoid the cords of the mikes and sound equipment snaking over the stage.

She joined Cam at his side and cameras flashed, blinding them both.

"Where do I look?" Dodie asked, as he slipped his arm around her. "What do I say?"

"Just smile and look around, gorgeous. And wave. You can say *danke schoen* if you really want them to go crazy."

She grinned and then, in accented German, leaned toward the mike. *"Ich danke dir sehr. Wir hatten eine tolle zeit hier."*

The crowd erupted at that, clapping even louder.

"Please tell me what you just said," he asked, his mouth by her ear so she could hear him in this deafening noise.

"I said thanks and said we had a great time."

"Where did you learn that?"

"Google Translate," she said. She turned toward the crowd, waving, smiling, the lights burnishing the perfect highlights in her hair.

"Have I told you how stunning you are?" he asked, pressing a kiss to her head.

"Not since the last break, handsome," she returned, lifting her face to his.

They heard the crowd chanting for them to kiss each other.

Something he never minded doing.

Then he waved to the audience again and stepped back from the mike.

"So, photos next?" Dodie asked, referring to the long-standing tradition of posing with pictures and signing autographs backstage with people who had paid for the privilege.

But Cam shook his head, relief flowing through him. "I told Gage that we're not doing that. I don't care if it's the last night. I want to get out of here. Back to the hotel. Grab a good night's sleep before we fly out."

Dodie tucked against him as they walked through the dim glow of the halls behind the stage toward their truck parked in a parkade that they could, thankfully, access from the auditorium.

"And then?" she asked, her tone teasing.

He stopped and held her shoulders, staring down at this amazing woman who had given up so much to be here with him. Who had made this entire tour so bearable. Who had never complained but had been amazed with all the things she had seen.

He saw the weariness etched in her face. Knew this tour had taken its toll on her. But it was over now.

"And then, my dear, amazing wife, we go home. Home to

Millars Crossing. Home to the farm. Home to all the stuff we have to do."

She sighed and kissed him again.

"I love the sound of that."

They walked away from the chanting crowd, the noise of the band playing one last tune as they headed to the truck.

Tomorrow they would head back to Millars Crossing.

Back home to start the next phase of their life together.

DID YOU LOVE MILLARS CROSSING?

CHECK out more stories in a different area - Aspen Valley.

WHEN HER BOYFRIEND broke up with her via text and her father destroyed her dreams of training barrel racing horses on their farm, Courtney left Aspen Valley, vowing never to return. She got married, had a baby and settled in the Netherlands. But a messy divorce and custody entanglements kept her overseas until her husband dies. Now her father wants her and her daughter, Fenna, to come back to Aspen Valley. It is guilt over her granddaughter being unable to see her grandfather that sends her reluctantly back home. Especially when she finds out Cole, her old boyfriend has become a veterinarian and is living there as well.

DURING HER TIME BACK, Fenna falls in love with the horses and farm life and doesn't want to go back to the Netherlands. However, when Courtney discovers her father is selling the farm she knows this means the horses Fenna adores will have to be sold as well. When her oldest barrel racing horse foals, it creates a time of bonding with her and her father. And Cole has been coming around, reigniting the old attraction. Just as she finds peace and redemption with her father and she and Cole are becoming closer, devastating secrets from the past rise up threatening both relationships. Can Courtney face the spectators from the past and find her way to love and forgiveness?

ESCAPE to Aspen Valley in *The Way Back Home*, a heartwarming and emotional story of the bonds of family, the cords of love and the peace forgiveness can give.

.

GET The Way Back Home

OTHER SERIES

I have many other books for you to enjoy. Check them out here.

LOVE IN MILLARS CROSSING

#1 A Family's Christmas

#2 A Family's Blessing

#3 A Family's Hope

#4 A Family's Promise (Coming soon)

MILLARS CROSSING ROMANCE

#1 COUNTRY ROMANCE

#2 COUNTRY COURTSHIP

#3 COUNTRY PROPOSAL

#4 COUNTRY WEDDING

FAMILY BONDS

#1 SEEKING HOME

A rancher who suffered a tragic loss. A single mother on the edge. Can these two find the courage to face a romantic new beginning?

#2 CHOOSING HOME

If you like emergency room drama, second chances, and quaint small-town settings, then you'll adore this romance.

#3 COMING HOME

He thought she chose a hotel over him. She thought he loved money more than her. Years later, can they fill the emptiness in their hearts?

#4 FINDING HOME

She's hiding a terrible truth. He's trying to overcome his scandalous history. Together, forgiveness might give them a second chance.

FAMILY TIES

Four siblings trying to finding their way back to family and faith

A COWBOY'S REUNION

He's still reeling from the breakup. She's ashamed of what she did. Can a chance reunion mend the fence, or are some hearts forever broken? If you like second chance stories, buried passions, and big country settings, then you'll love this emotional novel.

"I enjoyed this book and had trouble putting it down and had to finish it. If the rest of this series is this great, I look forward to reading more books by Carolyne Aarsen." Karen Semones - Amazon Review

THE COWBOY'S FAMILY

She's desperate. He's loyal. Will a dark lie hold them back from finding love on the ranch? If you like determined heroines, charming cowboys, and family dramas, then you'll love this heartfelt novel.

"What a wonderful series! The first book is Cowboy's Reunion. Tricia's story begins in that book. Emotional stories with wonderful characters. Looking forward to the rest of the books in this series." Jutzie - Amazon reviewer

TAMING THE COWBOY

A saddle bronc trying to prove himself worthy to a father who never loved him. A wedding planner whose ex-fiancee was too busy chasing his own dreams to think of hers. Two people, completely wrong for each other who yet need each other in ways they never realized. Can they let go of their own plans to find a way to heal together?

"This is the third book in the series and I have loved them all. . . . can't wait to see what happens with the last sibling." - Amazon reviewer

THE COWBOY'S RETURN

The final book in the Family Ties Series:

He enlisted in the military, leaving his one true love behind.

She gave herself to a lesser man and paid a terrible price.

In their hometown of Rockyview, they can choose to come together or say a final goodbye...

"This author did an amazing job of turning heartache into happiness with realism and inspirational feeling." Marlene - Amazon Reviewer

SWEETHEARTS OF SWEET CREEK

Come back to faith and love

#1 HOMECOMING

Be swept away by this sweet romance of a woman's search for belonging and second chances and the rugged rancher who helps her heal.

#2 - HER HEARTS PROMISE

When the man she once loved reveals a hidden truth about the past, Nadine has to choose between justice and love.

#3 - CLOSE TO HIS HEART

Can love triumph over tragedy?

#4 - DIVIDED HEARTS

To embrace a second chance at love, they'll need to discover the truths of the past and the possibilities of the future...

#5 - A HERO AT HEART

If you like rekindled chemistry, family drama, and small, beautiful towns, then you'll love this story of heart and heroism.

#6 - A MOTHER'S HEART

If you like matchmaking daughters, heartfelt stories of mending broken homes, and fixer-upper romance, then this story of second chances is just right for you.

HOLMES CROSSING SERIES

The Only Best Place is the first book in the Holmes Crossing Series.

#1 THE ONLY BEST PLACE

One mistake jeopardized their relationship. Will surrendering her dreams to save their marriage destroy her?

#2 ALL IN ONE PLACE

She has sass, spunk and a haunting secret.

#3 THIS PLACE

Her secret could destroy their second chance at love

#4 A SILENCE IN THE HEART

Can a little boy, an injured kitten and a concerned vet with his own past pain, break down the walls of Tracy's heart?

#5 ANY MAN OF MINE

Living with three brothers has made Danielle tired of guys and cowboys. She wants a man. But is she making the right choice?

#6 A PLACE IN HER HEART

Her new boss shattered her dreams and now she has to work with him. But his vision for the magazine she loves puts them at odds.

Can they find a way to work together or will his past bitterness blind him to future love.

Made in the USA
Middletown, DE
14 January 2023

22177461R00144